I0557909

OUR LEGEND
LIES WITH YOU

Lem Finney

Copyright © 2024 Lem Finney

All rights reserved

This is a work of fiction. Any references to historical
events, real people, or real places are used fictitiously. Other
names, characters, places, and incidents are products of
the author's imagination. Any similarity to actual persons,
living or dead, places, or events is entirely coincidental.

No part of this book may be reproduced, or stored in a
retrieval system, or transmitted in any form or by any
means, electronic, mechanical, photocopying, recording,
or otherwise, without express written permission of the
publisher.

ISBN: 979-8-9912308-1-0

Cover design by: Lem Finney
Printed in the United States of America

For Hayden—
For mourning them,
For loving me,
And letting me love you.

"YOU, Mary Read and Ann Bonny, alias Bonn, are to go from hence to the Place from whence you came, and from thence to the Place of Execution, where you shall be severally hang'd by the neck, 'till you are severally dead. And GOD of His infinite Mercy be merciful to both of your souls."

- SIR NICHOLAS LAWES, 1720
The Tryals of Captain John Rackam and other Pirates

"NOW we are to begin a History full of surprizing Turns and Adventures; I mean, that of Mary Read and Anne Bonny, alias Bonn, which were the true Names of these two Pyrates; the odd Incidents of their rambling Lives are such, that some may be tempted to think the whole Story no better than a Novel or Romance; . . . the Truth of it can be no more contested, than that there were such Men in the World, as Roberts and Black-beard, who were Pyrates."

- CAPTAIN CHARLES JOHNSON, 1724
A General History of the Robberies and Murders of the most notorious Pyrates

PROLOGUE

LEGENDS ARE AS REAL AS THE PEOPLE WHO CREATED THEM. They are stories living as truths in people's minds, but they serve their own selfish purposes. They only see what they want to see. Although, they cannot be truly blamed. They see through their lonely eyes and blindly believe what their biased brain tells them.

So let me be concise: I am not Anne Bonny.

That tale has been boiled down to an unrecognizable, pulsating mass. That damned '*Captain Johnson*' claimed some decade ago to have known that woman, making her into a sexual spectacle of female abnormality, abusing her life to sell some books. Yet, readers have eaten what has been fed to them, and it has become a part of them. And, in a way, they have made it into reality. When there are enough people sharing a collective conscience, when history has sided one way and left the other to dust, what voice remains whole and intact and unwavering amidst the sea of the mob to say it isn't true?

However, I do not write this for them.

This account is only for you. Only we need to know ourselves.

Yet, I am dying, dove, and I see my selfishness while writing this, lying sickly in bed: I want to stay with you in your memories, but as the woman *I* know myself as. I will not lie peacefully under the muddied paste of the earth knowing that my story also dies with me.

This, my story, *our story,* is as real as the other ones that have been distorted in this rippling pool of time. It is *our* legend because *they* believed in it, *she* believed in it, and for as long as I still breathe, I will believe in it. Believe in it, too. Believe in it for us.

This infamous Anne Bonny has been written about time and time again. She is nothing more than a passing breeze or a puff of dust, a shadow of what once was, but a myth still holds immense power over those who worship it. She has been made into a god or a faerie or a monster living off the edge of the map, lighting wild the imaginations of those captured by her tales. But enough has been said about them. I want to tell a different story.

To do that, allow me to dispel those myths about me:

I am not the fiery redhead from Cork.

I am not the hidden bastard of a Carolina plantation.

I am not the little girl raised in breeches as

her father's clerk.

I am not the crazed murderess of a servant.

I am not the loose wife of James Bonny.

I am not the vigorous lover of John Rackam.

I am not the disguised demon in men's clothes.

I am not the warrior woman who bears her breasts in battle.

I am not the mistress of the seas.

I am not the pirate queen.

I am not that legend.

I am only a woman.

My name is Ann Fulford.

TABLE OF CONTENTS

CHAPTER 1:

The Green Flash

THE SUN WAS SETTING ON OUR LAST DAY. Aye, it has been many years, but it was a beautiful sight, I remember: the sun was slipping into the endless watery horizon, hesitant, afraid the ocean would douse its light. When it touched the water, light spilled out in front of it like a cracked yolk, and it dissolved slowly into the soft rippling blue waves of the Caribbean in October.

I sat away from the crew alone with my legs dangling over the ship's bow. It wasn't a large ship, the *Mary*, being only a merchant sloop we stole some week or two prior, so I could clearly hear the men behind me slurring shanties arm-in-arm in drunken camaraderie as if inside my ear. We were in a secluded Jamaican cove not too far from what I would later learn was Negril-Point, and the crew decided it was an opportune time to carouse in good company. It was endearing, the unbridled joy they found in liquor and light revelry, and on another occasion I would have joined them, but I kept my back turned and my face towards the horizon. That was more important to me at the time.

Something warm was pressed to my side, and another pair of legs soon lay next to mine, dangling too over the steep drop into the dark sea below.

A flask of rum was held out to me.

"If you're going to brood alone, you might as well have a jag," Maura pestered me, a sly smile tugging at her lips.

"I am not brooding," I sneered at her without any real menace, but I took the offered drink anyway. "I am waiting."

"Fer what?"

"The green flash," I said to her before taking a swig of the liquid warmth without tearing my eyes away from the horizon.

We had been at sea for two months, and I had yet to see that infamous green flash. *The Green Hope*, sailors passing through smiled when buying their bread. *You'll ne'er go wrong in matters of the heart.* Some drunkards in taverns would mumble with sour breath into beer-soaked beards of some *poor sod* passing on to the other side of the light. *Glimpse you 'ere the green ray, count the 'morrow a fine day,* other grizzled mariners would muse while patching up old fishing nets. Perhaps it would bring me luck, perhaps it would bring me love, but I cared not for these gifts. Witnessing the natural majesty of a green light shooting across the sea was wondrous enough.

Maura chuckled softly, but not unkindly: "You and your legends, Ann." She took back the flask and tipped it back in her mouth.

My gaze broke away from the horizon as my eyes followed her movements. She hissed between her teeth at the booze's bite, but her dark eyes sparkled with a gay and lively mirth when they met mine. Her naturally dark complexion deepened through years of sun exposure, toughening the skin around her eyes into a crinkled leather. Whenever she smiled, the lines on her face wrote out a piece of her past.

"I'm still unused to your cropped hair." Maura had cut her brown hair short like a man's a few days before. They were fine scissors, the ones she used. Real silver blades with swirling designs that we plundered from a passing sloop.

"What, don't you like it?" She teased me with a smirk, but some need for approval glimmered in her eyes.

"I never said I didn't. I just said I'm not used to it." Without the extra locks weighing them down, soft natural ringlets framed her face like a halo. I allowed Maura a small smile, and hummed once I reached a consensus. "I've decided I like it. It suits you, I think.

A thud rattled the wooden planks we sat on, making the two of us turn around to survey the ruckus. A barrel had been knocked over with our dear Captain John Rackam lying flat on his back next to it. John had apparently tried to hop onto it, but he had misjudged his jump and toppled over, bringing the barrel down with him. If he had been hurt, he didn't mind it. He sat back up, giggling, with a dark olive green bottle in his hand. When he spotted me looking at him with a raised brow, he called everyone to his attention.

"Everyone, everyone! I propose a song, *a song!* for my own Bonny lass, my darling *Bonny Ann!*" John held his bottle towards me in cheers, while I rolled my eyes at the nickname he gave me. He laughed at this with more force than what a laugh should have had and nearly coughed out his innards. He carefully stood back up, uprighted the barrel, and sat on it before swinging out his hands, as if to conduct his orchestra of drunks.

"*My Bonny lies over the ocean,*" John began, less singing and more shouting with a voice sore from all the other songs. "*My Bonny lies over the sea . . .* "

The others caught on and joined his song, swaying to the rhythm as voices of all pitches grated on each other:

"*My Bonny lies over the ocean,*
So bring back my Bonny to me!
Bring back, bring back,
Bring back my Bonny to me, to me!

Bring back, bring back,
Bring back my Bonny to me, to me!"

They laughed heartily, their shoulders shaking and faces reddening. Rat Nose would have tipped over if it weren't for the Admiral pressed to his side, propping him up. Seagull and Handsome Dick saw all of this nearby, and they both barked with laughter at the boy's inability to hold his booze. They all began to sing again, but Maura and I turned away from them.

The sun was about halfway down, and my lips were pressed into a line as straight as the horizon before us. Maura nudged me with a foot.

"How are things with you and Rackum?"

I shrugged. "They're all right, I suppose. I mean, nothing has changed. He keeps pestering me to come to his quarters with promises of wine and some nice smelling perfumes—rose and that, like, weird whale shit—but, I don't know, Maura . . . I just don't want to. I keep turning him down. I like the guy, he's my friend and all, but he just wants to strum me, not really love me. Even if I wanted a shag, I can't imagine myself waking up in his arms. He's exhausted most of the men on the ship, so he wants to change it up with a woman. I'm not in the mood to be played like that."

Maura hummed in agreement. "That's how it was for me and Andrew. He was fun for a good bugger now and again, but even that was soon ruined for me when he opened his mouth in the morn. Take it from me; love someone who'll be by your side in bed *and* in battle."

I nodded solemnly. "I'm sorry for what happened between you two."

"Don't be. That son-of-a-bitch was a waste of good rum and salted fish. Just wish he had the balls to leave us sooner. Now, he can do whatever he damn-well pleases. See if I care."

Maura took another harsh drink as nonchalantly as she could, but the hard press of her lips on the valve told me that some small part of her still did care. She pressed the flask back in my hands, and I took a sip.

The singing died down and its voices dispersed into idle chatter and full-belly laughs. We looked back to the limitless expanse of the water and sat in comfortable, companionable silence. The sky behind the sun was a dark, dusty orange and beyond that was a rosy red. Maura distracted me when she began to swing her feet slightly back and forth, and I swung them in time with her. It was just her and me and the sea. We turned to each other with soft grins and giggled at ourselves.

When we turned back to the horizon, only a sliver of the sun remained.

"So," Maura asked, "what are we looking fer?"

"When the sun drops, there should be a burst of green light, a green flash or whatever. A ray. Hope. Something like that?"

"What the hell does that look like? Does the

Sun, what, shoot a beam into the sky, as if to call the angels of the Lord?"

"I don't know, Maura. That's why I'm waiting to find out."

I darted my eyes to her in exasperation and just as quickly redirected my stare back to their subject. Without knowing, I leaned forward on the ship's wooden railing as the sun dipped further and further into the ever-growing inky emerald depths that were swallowing it whole. It was about to fall under the tide when Maura gave a loud startled gasp.

My head immediately snapped to her, looking for danger, as I quickly sputtered out: "What, what's wrong?"

She was simply smiling ahead with broad teeth, the last remnants of light dancing in her eyes. "Oh, I just saw it! Yea, I saw—och, what'd you call it?—the green flash!"

"What! Where?" I nearly yelled, whipping my head around and scanning the horizon. Alas, I saw nothing but the afterglow of a sunset, the sun dead and gone.

"Aw, you just missed it!"

I turned back to Maura, who was side-eyeing me, trying to compose the grin threatening to spread across her face.

"Oh, you bastard!" I said as I shoved her back onto the wooden planks of the deck. She had the gall to laugh at me. "You distracted me! I bet you didn't even see it."

"I did, I did, I swear!" Maura repeated, holding up her hands in honest surrender as she sat back up, but her burst of giggles made her look like the victor of this meager battle.

"Oh, but you should have seen the look on your face. Looked like an owl . . . hoo-hee-hee," she wheezed and squeezed her sides. "Like an owl, swiveling its head around. Startled by a gunshot . . . " She put a hand over her mouth to attempt to suppress her laughter. It did not work. "Your face is almost as red as your hair right now."

"Maura!"

"Sorry, sorry, but I had to! It was too tempting. You were wound up like a clock. I s'pose you'll just have to make due with the poetics I'll wax about it in *excruciating* detail." She leaned close to me, mocking sincerity as her lips enunciated each hefty word. "Would that s'fice?"

I narrowed my eyes at her in response.

"Oh, come now. Don't be like that. I really did see it. Believe me?"

She cocked her head at me and studied me like a questioning cat. Her wide eyes were as dark as the night sky creeping above us, and they reflected the lone Evening Star, *Venus,* having just poked its head out in the Sun's absence. I couldn't refute those eyes that shone with such honest affection.

"All right. I'll believe you."

We smiled at each other, and some new ribbon of understanding had begun to wrap itself around us, perhaps forever.

And just as suddenly as it came to be, that silent, tender peace between us was broken by the loud boom of a gun fire, and I don't think either of us ever found it again.

Jostled, Maura and I steadied ourselves and looked over to the commotion. There, we saw the smoke wafting into the air from a rifle. It seemed to be pointing towards a passing merchant sloop, but more dangerously, a naval ship was approaching it from behind. No Knees Davies, as if controlled by some instinctive apparition, came to and lowered the gun, clutching its barrel to his chest with gnarled hands.

"You old *fool!*" Rackum shouted, staggering across the ship over to him in a moment of either sober determination or drunken rage. Davies had broad shoulders and a bulky figure despite his being the oldest of the crew, but he lost some of his imposing nature with his short peg legs, allowing Rackum to tower over him menacingly. He grabbed Davies by his tattered tunic and lifted the man off his wooden feet. He looked so small with his shoulders hunched in terror.

"I-I'm sorry, cap'n," he babbled, "but it's the English!"

"And we had half a chance to be passed by 'em without our bloody colors flying!" Rackum threw Davies to the ground. I winced when his back slammed on the planks.

"All hands on deck!" Rackum screamed in

his breaking lungs, pacing around the ship. "Rat Nose, Dobbins, unfurl the masts! Seagull, take the wheel. The rest of you lot, prepare any guns and weapons you can!"

The crew scattered in all directions as Rackum made his way to stand squarely beside the helm. Seagull spun the wheel next to him once the masts were loose and directed our ship out of the cove. Everyone sobered within a moment's notice as if they had never drunk a drop a day in their lives.

I still remember John's face. His greasy, sun-tainted hair fell out of its braid, sweeping the tense angle of his jaw. His black tricorn cast a dark shadow over his furrowed brow. As his lips tightened into a stiff line, I could feel my own teeth beginning to grind. His posture was unnatural. Perhaps he tried to make himself appear intimidating—surely aiming for calm, but sorely missing the mark—to save face for the crew. He stood with his feet apart, his sweaty hands pressed into fists behind his back, trembling despite his feigned confidence. His eyes drooped, the whites burning into a bloodshot red. Every broken capillary spelled out the doubt that plagued his mind: *you're weak, John.*

Maura and I rushed below deck and passed out whatever pistols or muskets or sheathed swords we had among our crew. When they frantically pried them from our grips, we ran back up to the open air to stand guard on deck. Maura and I each hung a sword belt and a pistol on our waists and walked out with an additional musket in our hands. We then joined the rest of our crew above.

After the naval sloop had pulled alongside the merchant's, it began to tear through the waves after us. We sailed along the coast on our left, hoping to stay close to the shore in hopes of throwing it off. Many of us, Maura and myself included, leaned over the ship's side to make something out of the ship that gave chase. There wasn't much to behold for the only light we had was from the pale yellow glow of the long-gone sunset, struggling to fight against the deep blue current of night that strangled it. Little lights dotted the naval ship's bow, but ours remained in the dark.

"Don't let anybody light our lanterns!" Rackum called out. "The darkness will cloak our movements. We sail by the light of the waning moon."

The moon's place in the sky told me that it was roughly ten o'clock at night when the sloop caught up with us. They were on our tail for a few hours, and each of them was spent by every one of us waiting anxiously for the next move, looking desperately for a way we could escape them without confrontation. We could overtake a merchant sloop or a fishing boat with our plundered goods, but we were no match for the Crown's endless resources, and we prayed to whatever God there was for a miracle. However, He refused to listen to the likes of us, and no such luck came.

The speed of the English ship granted them the grace to sidle up beside us. Realizing our fate, we stopped to face them, and they hailed our ship. Rackum ushered us to take up our battle stations in preparation.

"Who is your captain?" called out a voice that, when leaning over the ship's rail, I could vaguely discern belonged to a young man in a polished uniform, cream and blue coat illuminated by the orange glow of sea lanterns.

"John Rackum," Rackum answered hoarsely. "Of Cuba."

"John Rackam?" a different voice responded, heavy and incredulous before laughing, gruff and smug. "Ha! It's Jonathon, Jonathon Barnet!"

Even in the dark, I saw the blood flood into Rackum's face.

"Do they know each other?" Maura whispered beside me.

"A past privateer, perhaps?" I responded, unsure. "They sailed the same seas for an age, after all."

"Och, of *course.* You reckon they were banging bollox before or after his pardon?"

"Shut *up,* Maura."

"And where is that oafish pennon you swore to never sail under again?" the man continued after his men had laughed, "I am proud to wave the colors of the sovereign King of England. By all means, traitors, strike immediately upon our flag that frightens you so."

John looked as if his eyes were about to pop out of his sockets as he rushed down the ship's steps. I knew I had to divert control away from him if we wanted to get out of this mess alive, so I leaned over the ship's taffrail and called out:

"We will not strike!"

Too late: Rackum swung a loaded swivel gun to face the naval vessel. He fired, cannonball striking the ship immediately and sending a row of men on deck flying backwards.

"John!" I cried, bitter and desperate, but he was back to reloading the gun, deaf to my warning.

"Broadside!" Barnet roared in reply, and gunports in their ship lifted their trapdoors to reveal a line of cannons being pushed out, facing directly at our ship.

"Get the cannons!" Maura bent down and yelled below our deck to the few men stationed there. I heard the crackling of chains as our sloop's gunports were raised.

"Volley!" Barnet ordered, and two lines of soldiers formed. The front bent down on one knee, and the second standing tall and unmoving, the silver of their smoothbore muskets pointing directly at us glistening in the dim oil light. "Ready . . . "

"Fire. Fire now!" I hollered to the men around me. "Anyone! Catch them off-guard!"

Maura was the first to fire her musket. I watched her bullet hit the shoulder of a man in the second row, knocking him off his feet. I fired mine and it hit someone in the hip and sent him sinking to the ground. More scattered shots on our side followed at random, picking off the English little by little before Barnet had the chance to give his orders of English pageantry.

"Aim . . . "

Our swivel guns and cannons then came after, blowing a good chunk of a gunport away below and dispersing a third of the English men above. We had the advantage of chaos and being of little numbers, spaced out on the deck, as opposed to their dense, rigid formation.

But their captain grew impatient.

"Fire!"

An onslaught of cannons and gunfire came all at once, ripping a wooden gash in our deck and a second on the ship's side. I was knocked to the ground on impact just as a bullet whispered above my head. It flew past me instead, splintering through the cap of Cathy's knee behind me. He fell to the ground and cradled his knee to his chest, screaming.

A steady hand gripped my bicep and hoisted me up on my feet. It was Maura.

"No time to think," she told me, or perhaps she was telling herself. "No time to die."

She brought a hand to her hips, pulled out her pistol, and held it out in front of her within the span of a breath. She closed one eye, quickly aimed, and fired. It hit a frontman straight in the head and killed him.

The English of the other sloop lifted a large plank together and laid it across the rails of our ships, creating a bridge. They began to march across. I lifted my pistol and fired, hitting a man dumbly in the shin, but enough to unbalance him and send him plummeting into the water, and bringing another man with him.

But we couldn't stop them. More and more came until our sloop was swarming with them. Maura and I fought side by side with our blades and whatever ammo we had left. I had never seen Maura so ferocious, fighting with bloody tooth and nail as if she was an ocelot cornered by malicious hunters, protecting the very skin she wore. I don't suppose I was any better. If she was a feral cat, snarling and pushing and plunging head-first into danger without regard for herself, with both nothing and everything to lose, then I was a viper, slipping in and out of my victims and striking at whatever opening that lay defenseless.

I don't remember much of that battle. The memory is clouded by the smoke of guns and masked by the metallic taste of steel on steel. My body fought while my mind floated up into the smoky air somewhere.

I was not a good fighter. Lord, no. I wasn't trained, not in the Navy like the Admiral or Davies, and neither had I any swashbuckling legacy like

Rackum or even Little Fen.

But I was determined to live, so I did; I had to win, so I won. It was as simple as that. No thought was spared for the risks and repercussions, for what came after the blood and the broken bones.

I had earned a large gash while facing off another man. He extended his sword, his right side vulnerable, so I angled my sword from below with my left hand, extended, and stabbed through his liver. I then maneuvered my body just enough for my opponent's sword to merely scrape my side. The large, scathing slash was big enough to leave me stumbling and struggling to hold up my sword, yet I still stood upright while my opponent fell to his knees.

All I knew was survival. All I knew was the fear of losing what I had just gained. We were only on the sea for less than *two months,* for Christ's sake! It's almost laughable to think about it now, how the taste of a two-monthed life drove us into a willing destruction.

The end felt so near when this life had only just begun. But, God, were we tired and *woefully* outnumbered.

Many of the crew had already been captured by the English. Out of the corner of my eye, I saw Jackie Iron flailing under the pressing weight of two English officers as his hands were being bound by rope. He bit the arm of one of the men, which earned him a yelp and a punch in the face from the navy sailor. Blood sputtered from his nose and his eyes rolled over into unconsciousness.

I felt a force tackle me from behind and pin me to the ground as a breathy *oomph* escaped my lips. A knee pressed into my open wound as the man began to tie my hands, and I felt my vulnerable flesh ooze with blood upon his cotton pant. I cried out in pain.

"Don't you feckin' *touch her!*" I heard Maura's voice above all others, and a sudden force was briefly added until it was entirely lifted. I craned my neck over my shoulder to see Maura on the back of my assailant, arm wrapped tightly around his neck and making his pudgy, sunburnt face turn violet and green.

A different sailor came into view and hit Maura square on the back with his musket, loosening her hold on him just enough for the officer to quickly whip his body around and have her thrown off his back. The officer grabbed her on the ground, briskly turned her on her belly, and pressed her snugly beside me. As the other sailor came up to me to tighten my bonds, Maura squirmed and yelled and kicked with all of her might, but with all of the large officer's weight pushing down upon her, she accomplished nothing.

I heard every scream ring in my ears, some in rage, some in fear, some in delirious triumph. Blood was sprayed to my right, but I did not know whose. My body trembled; with blood loss, dread, or death, I did not know. I could only feel its involuntary convulsions.

Nothing can be done, I thought, squeezing my bulging eyes shut. My eyelashes stung like little pins in my eyes. *We're finished.*

"Quarter!" I heard someone cry. I strained my neck to see the voice's owner, John Rackum, pressed weaponless against the stairs with a sword to his throat. "Quarter for me and my crew!"

The man holding the sword laughed, and even from only his back, I knew him to be that same Captain Barnet who gave the orders to his men: "Lord Above, John, do I take that as a surrender from the infamous pirate Captain Rackam?"

Rackum clenched his jaw and muttered a forced "yes."

Staring in disbelief at Barnet, I saw his large shoulders bounce by his ears. He was chuckling.

"You are a coward once again," Barnet said mostly to himself, but he did not care if his words were on full display. He shouted to his sailors while taking Rackum by the shoulders and throwing him down onto the deck to tie up his hands: "Mark this day for history, men! The pride of John Rackam has faltered, and he has relinquished his life and his crew to the gibbets. Round up the rest who haven't been tied up already."

I heard swords drop and men laughing and cheering as bodies thudded onto the wooden planks. The sailor had finished tying my hands, and he focused his attention on restraining

Maura with the officer. Even though her hands were bound, she still continued to writhe uncontrollably beneath them. Her teeth bared like fangs when she screamed. Her hardened eyes were red and raw with salty tears threatening to spill. Somehow, her pupils seemed smaller and more intense in a predatory stare fixed upon the men behind her, caught in a haze of vengeance.

"Maura, *Maura!*" I called out to her. This got her to freeze, and her eyes turned to me, and in that pause, I could truly see the fear she hid within her.

"Stop fighting," I told her with a sad smile. I mustered all of my remaining energy to lean over as far as I could to press my elbow to her arm, even though my chemise stretched awkwardly against the salt-slicken deck. I felt the eyes of the men on top of Maura regarding us incredulously. "It's over."

Her face contorted and whatever spell that was cast on her had completely broken, and only sorrow took its place. A gray haze was encroaching on my vision, but through it, there was the white sparkle of a small tear on Maura's face. It rolled down her cheek and fell through the cracks of the planks it was pressed against.

"Lord Almighty," I heard the sailor above me utter in awe. My head rolled towards his voice, and through my shutting eyes, I followed his gaze leading to my tunic. The strings that had tightened it across my bust were loosened, and the sticky planks beneath were chafing my exposed pale breast.

"It's a woman," he gawked, but it was fading into space, like an echo.

"They both are," remarked the other voice, but it was spinning far away. "How peculiar."

I forgot the world around me. Gradually, I felt the heavy weight of sleep push me through the ground. I gladly fell into the darkness beneath.

CHAPTER 2:

Spanish-Town Gaol

I WAS SITTING AT THE BOTTOM OF THE SEA, *and I knew I was dead. I can remember that much. My hair was floating above me in bright orange tendrils, swaying like a flickering flame in the ocean currents, but it was all tainted blue by the faraway sunlight piercing through the water. I held a teacup in my hand, bright white china with pink roses. There was a table before me with lace doilies; biscuits and small sandwiches floated above the plates and trays with my cup's matching pattern. I reached out to grab a morsel of food (when was the last time I was ever fed?) but a warty claw caught my wrist. It belonged to the devil sitting across from me, smiling at me. It had bright red hair like mine, and I pushed myself away, falling through the soft sand of the ocean floor.*

When I woke up, I was gasping for air, like I

had been drowning. The suddenness of my breath sent a sharp pain through my body, and I groaned through my clenched teeth.

"Oy, oy, oy," whispered a kind voice, and a smiling face came fluttering into my view. It was Maura's. "Don't strain yourself. Please."

My senses were slowly restored to me, and I ceased my struggling. Maura had my head resting on her lap instead of being left on the thin clump of straw beneath our bodies. The room was dark, but the little illumination came through the only barred window, too high to reach. Shadows of dark blue lines were cast across the floor from the pale moonlight.

"Where . . . " my voice trailed off, my voice scratchy and slow. "What happened?"

"We were arrested by the English. They dumped us ashore at Davis's Cove in the hands of some lickarse Major, James-something. But, they did have someone there to patch you up."

This prompted me to glance at my body, heavily bandaged in the middle. A dark maroon stain still came through on my left, but it looked dry enough.

When I looked back up at Maura, her back slumped against the wall, her face was still roughly the same, save for the long scar, crusty red turning scabbish brown, that stretched from her throat to her jaw, but I could see that something had changed. Her cheeks were drawn out, almost sagging on her high cheekbones without the propping of her constant teasing grin. Her brown skin, no longer warm with the sun and her merriment, had a sickly undertone to it.

"You were out fer three days," she whispered, her voice light with airy delirium. Her eyes, darkened with sobriety, drifted over my face before tucking away a stray lock of hair that clung to my sweaty forehead. Her mind worked behind her expressionless eyes, deciding among too many things to say, before settling on:

"I missed you."

My bottom lip trembled at the evident anxiety that lined every part of her sunken face. I wanted to apologize for making her worry about me, but the words that rushed through my throat only choked me, and I coughed.

Maura mumbled something and turned away to produce a crude tin cup from her side. Her cool yet calloused hand slipped under my burning neck and lifted my head gently to the rim. "Here," she said blankly, "drink this."

I could not say no to her frantic eyes, so I obeyed her wish and drank. It must have been a poorly brewed beer. Other things swam with it in my mouth, and there was a stale saltiness to it, but my throat was too parched to complain.

"They schedule our meals and our drinks, our keepers." I drank slowly, but Maura was patient with me and talked in between my sips. "They come twice a day, around breakfast and supper, I'd say. They have given me a drink and some dry, God-awful bread. Although, they only gave enough fer myself, so I've had to ration enough fer the both of us while you were gone."

I stopped drinking once my body had hit its limit. Maura took it away with a pitying look and leaned my head back down. "It's closer to piss than beer, probably, with the color of neither. Sorry for that. I do have some food for you, but perhaps we'll save that for the morning."

The sparse moonlight of the early hours of the morning cloaked our surroundings in a cool darkness, but if I squinted well enough, I could see the dense bricks that made up the holdout. Iron grates divided the space into cells, two on each side of the walkway cutting down the middle. Maura and I were put alone in the one at the far end of the row, furthest from the large wooden door on the other side.

"They took us to Saint Jago de la Vega," Maura pronounced the Spanish name with ease. From what I gleaned, she was taught it young by her father, sparingly though. She knew enough phrases to string together a sentence, but not enough where it came naturally to her. Besides, her father never seemed home long enough after to have a full conversation with, Spanish or otherwise. Despite that, her pronunciation was always very smooth to my untrained ears, but still, the name she spoke was foreign to me.

"Spanish-Town Gaol," she answered the quizzical look I gave her. "That's where we're at now, and we'll stay here until our trial."

I nodded, but the knowledge did not soothe me: I longed to know where the rest of our crew was. A needling fear whispered to me that they were all dead, killed in battle or hung without trial. There were lumps of sleeping bodies in the other cells, or at least bodies pretending and praying for sleep, but I couldn't make out anyone's forms.

"John . . . " I croaked as my eyes darted frantically.

Maura's eyes faltered, looking away from my face towards the other cells around us. "He's here. He's all right, along with the rest of the crew. We were all fairly marked up, except dear ol' Rackum. He's mostly in one piece while the rest of us are in shambles."

"Idiot . . . " I muttered. "Great big . . . dog booby . . . "

"Yes, yes, I know," she scoffed. "He's in that cell, over there—" she pointed to the cell on the other side, closest to the door, "—but he hasn't spoken to anyone since he sucked up to that Barnet fellow. Barely touches his food after his pride was *so* wounded."

Maura grinned smugly without a drop of remorse. She and John had never been on the best terms for reasons that escaped me. John was a hard one to love and very few of us could stomach him, but he was still our captain and we gave him as much respect as we could, but Maura was never afraid to speak plainly about him. *Coward,* she wanted to say by the way she clenched her jaw, but around me, she held her tongue.

She wanted to die there, fighting on the *Mary*, rather than die here in Spanish-Town. I saw it then in her fiery resistance in the battle, and I saw it again in her chilling resentment in our cell. She felt robbed, not of glory, but the chance to die for the life she loved.

Perhaps John was a coward. Perhaps I should have died in a blaze on that ship. Perhaps I should have felt grateful for being given a little time to say *adieu* to Maura and my friends. But I didn't feel anything.

"You . . . " I took a breath to continue, " . . . well?"

Maura's eyes crinkled when I asked that. My panting question revealed the kind of light that used to glow in her eyes when we were together, before our imposing fate had come to smother it. The air became easier to breathe after she looked at me that way. Her eyes are what always settled me.

"Well, besides the chunk of my leg that had been blown to bits, I'm just grand." My eyes went wide when I turned to look over her legs stretched out before her. Her left one was heavily bandaged, and there seemed to be a large dent on the back of her calf. Maura's chuckle rippled from her stomach and rumbled through my ears. She turned my face back towards hers and said: "It's only a patch of muscle, Ann. All will be well. Fret not."

The plain tenderness on my friend's face

settled me and lulled me into a comfort, despite the stone and straw that bit through my back. For the first time in many days, there was safety in the air with Maura's attention hovering over me. She would take care of me, I was sure of it. That trust granted me the ease of fatigue, and I could feel a heaviness blanketing my eyes.

Startled by my sudden fade in energy, Maura's smile suddenly dropped, and her gaze darted across my face for any sign that I would slip away.

"Wait, Ann, please," Maura choked on a dry throat, "You can't ... don't leave me."

Perhaps she was anxious for my death, but I felt warm and alive from her endearing sentiment. I tried to reassure her as she did with me. I spoke what I could, trying to pace myself in between words to not overexert myself:

"I will ... " I paused to catch my breath, " ... wake ... tomorrow." I couldn't help but smile and repeat her words: "Fret not."

Maura released a sigh, and her shoulders sunk into their previous slouch against the wall, but the thin, long arms that held me were still stiff, cautious. The tautness in her body could not be completely relieved, but I promised to come back, and the sight of her half-lidded eyes as I began to doze led me to believe I gave Maura some small reprieve.

This time, sleep was of safety and comfort, not of escape. I could faintly feel the ghost of cold fingers dancing through my hair.

* * *

BEING IN A PRISON IS LIKE BEING UNDERWATER; you're submerged and surrounded by isolation where sounds are muffled, far away, and unimportant. Time becomes a passing thought, a thing invented by a world beyond the surface you are no longer privy to, a world that has left you to drown and die. You try to move, but your arms can hardly push against the weight of water, and all you can manage is to float along the soft currents and hold your breath. The only sign that life still persists at all is the billowing ribbons of sunlight that slice through the sea.

That was the first thing I saw when I woke up: the sunlight, piercing through the bars of our window and streaking across the walls of the cell opposite of us. I could only wonder what lived outside. I wasn't awake when they brought me in. I had no perception of where we were. *There is a world out there that I cannot see,* I thought, and I wondered if I would ever see it again. Perhaps the moment they were to lead us out of these living tombs to the cite stage, I would meet the endless horizon I yearned for one last time.

We were going to be hung, that was certain. There was no way to escape it. Trials for those in the colonies were only considered a theatrical performance to the English anyway, but for us, they wanted blood. We had no defense, no witnesses to advocate for us—but what was there to advocate anyway? We had broken their laws, we killed their men, what was left? What was left was to wait until our inevitable demise.

When the day was bad, my mum would tell me to go to sleep, and in the morning light, everything would appear better.

The light of day failed to make our situation any more pleasant. It only highlighted its obscenity.

In the daylight, I could plainly see how vulgar the cell was. That was a feat in of itself, for I had lived some months on a ship where chamber pots would roll around with every crash of a wave, splattering its contents across the rocking floor.

But here, there were ghosts. I wondered how many people vomited here, how many shat here, how many died and deteriorated and became one with the walls and floors. I wondered if I would be added to that list.

There was not enough room in the little window for the sun's warmth to infiltrate the chamber, but the walls were thick enough to trap the heat and humidity within. It was still dark, the air was dense, and the walls were still clammy and cool from the night before, but there was a warmth behind my head, and it grounded me.

My head still rested against her leg from where I was last night, and slouched against the wall was Maura with her head drooped above me in sleep. Her wide mouth was parted slightly, and she breathed evenly. Her long dark lashes fanned out against her skin, but there was movement behind her eyelids; she was dreaming. I could only hope that it was peaceful.

I slid away from her and leaned up, slowly, as to not budge her from her position, but pain shot from my wound to my body in protest. I pressed on, and took many deep, slow breaths once I righted myself. This caught the attention of someone:

"Move anymore, and you'll bust that seam across your skin."

I rolled my eyes and mocked, "Good morrow to you, Dobbins. It's nice to see you still breathing, Dobbins."

"I'd rather keep your spleen from spilling out on the floor, Bonny Ann, than exchange niceties."

I turned my head to him, and there was Dobbins, pressed against the iron dividing us. He was a man of scraggly hair, bleached blond by the sun, and a scruffy beard to match. He hailed all the way from Philadelphia. He could have been lying when he told us—half of us lied about our past, anyway—but his lips wrapped themselves strangely around certain words. The vowels were English, long and lazy on his tongue, but the R's turned coarse and rugged behind his teeth. Perhaps that part was Dutch, but I had no comparison.

I inched my way past Maura to sit by him beside the grate. It was a slow process, dragging my body about some six feet across the jagged floor, and once I used all of my energy to reach the border of the small cell, I huffed and leaned back, closing my eyes.

"Are you already tired of three full days of sleep?" He joked.

"Shut up."

Dobbins chuckled, but I knew beyond that nonchalant exterior, he was worried, even about me. He couldn't fool me. After a month or so with the man, I learned his patterns: that's how he expressed any sort of gratitude or affection or concern—through jokes.

"Are you hurt?" I asked, wanting to show that his friendly worries were not one-sided.

"Yea, some blunderbuss shot straight through my foot." He gestured to his bare, bandaged foot that lay limp against the other still in its boot. "Got a hole in there now, I think. I couldn't bear to look at it, so I dunno for sure. I let Woody patch it up for me.

Looking past Dobbins, I saw Woody asleep on the floor behind him, legs tucked to his chest like a cat's. His large mop of brown hair was tied away from his face, but a few curls escaped and covered his face.

I don't think a single one of us knew much of anything about Woody. He was mute and mostly deaf as far as we could tell, so he couldn't really volunteer many stories of who he was or where he came from in the first place.

However, for as long as I had known him, he wore a golden chain around his neck. There was a pendant attached to it, but it plunged beneath his collarbone into the folds of his plain starchy tunic where I couldn't make out what it was. In quiet moments when the waves would bob our ship up and down, lulling some to sleep or others to vomit, I would often see him gazing longingly at the ghosts of islands dotting the hazy horizon. Then, he would reach his spindly fingers into his tunic in search of his pendant to clutch tightly in a balled fist and kiss it tenderly.

With how he sometimes crossed himself in the sort of way Catholics did before we would enter a raid, I thought for the longest time it was some sort of rosary like the one my mother used to wear. I don't think my mother would have considered herself Catholic though, so I think it was something left over from someone in her family who might have been, but I'm unsure about this; she never spoke of her family—or, I suppose, *my* family. Nevertheless, she would always let it hang proudly on her bosom like some sort of medal of unwavering faith. It was crudely carved out of wood at one point, but its jagged job had been worn down by my mother's nervous fingers that had run over it time and time again. Even with its poor state, she would never let me touch it when I asked. I couldn't understand why a piece of rubbish would be so important.

Maybe it was this curiosity towards something I was never able to grasp that led me to quietly walk to Woody's side, unnoticed by the crew as he leaned against the prow in one of his moments of recollection. In my poor attempt at communication, I pointed towards his chest and used my hands to mimic a necklace hanging around my throat. He must have understood something in my wild gestures for he looked at me with a blank earnesty before wordlessly pulling his necklace over his head and handing it to me. It wasn't a rosary at all; it was a cameo.

"Is this your girl?" I whispered, like it was some sacrilegious thing to speak loudly. I soon remembered he couldn't hear me, so I pointed between the cameo-girl and himself.

He seemed to understand, and he nodded without looking at me. He was staring at the pale ivory profile against the crimson background. The woman depicted must have been fairly young at the time it was made, or perhaps the artist took some liberties in carving her likeness, and perhaps its holder didn't mind the deviations. It was meant to serve as a symbol rather than an exact copy; it was that which was represented that mattered. My mother must have felt the same about her rugged rosary. Their symbols served the same purpose.

Despite rarely going to mass, and despite her frowned-upon livelihood, my mother clung fast to her cross to remind the world or, more pressingly, to remind *herself* that she was worth a damn in someone's eyes, in *His* eyes, maybe. I think that is what kept her afloat in some dire straits. Or else, I might have completely lost her to the relentless tide of a burdensome world.

I thought if you devoted yourself to God, He would save you from the temptations of this world. Evil, wretched things, tainted by our errant brother, the Devil. But you were already born bad —I, probably born worse than others—and you had to apologize to Him every day and repent by living His doctrine. You love Him; you beg Him to love you. You owe your life; He *owned* your life. You were born into your sin, long before your mother bore you. He created and doomed your blood from the beginning. *The Indentured Servant of God.*

No, I didn't want to be devoted to anything. I wanted my life to be my own. However lonely and uncertain it may be, I wanted to free myself of devotion.

But wasn't Woody also devoted to his love? He held his mass whenever he clutched his cameo. Woody prayed to his lover, *for* his lover; she was the power he wished upon. And that seemed to keep him afloat on some of the bleakest days of our sailing, so perhaps devotion existed beyond God.

What did I pray for? What did I wish upon? What did I believe in? Nothing came up. In my own moment of recollection, I was just as lost as I had always been, now with nothing to run from and nowhere to run to. It was only this empty chasm called a gaol, this void we were *all* thrown into. None of us had anything left, nothing to claim or call our own.

The English had taken away Woody's cameo. They had confiscated anything we allegedly had no use for, anything that wasn't a piece of clothing to preserve our modesty. Without it, what would Woody have to pray on? What kept Woody from drowning now?

As I was searching for an answer that evaded me, I didn't realize Dobbins was still speaking:

" . . . have a few scratches otherwise, but nothing I'm not used to."

"Is he doing well?"

Dobbins glanced behind him at Woody. "Him? Oh, yea, for the most part. Got manhandled pretty rough when they were rounding us up. Some bastard bashed his head into the planks. He's got a large bruise up on his forehead, but it's healing up. Got a nasty scratch along his arm, though. But it might form into a wicked scar in some time," he smiled sadly, "but I don't really know how much time we've got."

With our death so imminent, there, I wondered, *did it matter?* What good could purpose and prayer bring now? Alas, I did not have an answer to my life; why should I find one now? We were all set to *shake a cloth in the wind*. Neither God nor Love could save us then.

Devotion has failed us, I thought. It would save no one in the end, and the end was drawing nigh; I had no time left to regret never converting.

Dobbins's eyes were downcast on his hands that rested openly on his lap, like he didn't know what to do with them. Through the grate, I tentatively reached out my hand to gently squeeze his shoulder. I don't think he was used to supportive touch, especially when he had not asked for it, because he flinched with the contact. However, he brought his hand up to mine without looking and patted it tenderly in appreciation. When he pulled away, so did I.

"How's Cathy?"

"He's recovering all right, but I doubt he'll be able to walk well anymore. They got the bullet out of his knee, so he was able to keep the leg, miraculously, but it could go sour at any moment, so I dunno for how long. Not that he'll need it, where we're going . . . " Dobbins trailed away for a moment before bringing himself back out of his daze. "The Admiral's taking good care of him. Too good. It's sickening to see him dote on Cathy." They were curled up in the corner of their cell, Cathy asleep on the Admiral's chest with the Admiral's arms wrapped around him. His eyes were open, the jolting blue of his irises poking through his dark lashes, but they were only on Cathy. He had no desire to join the conversation. He rarely did.

The Admiral had never been much of a conversationalist, even when I first met him during Rackum's recruitment in Providence. We only learned of his sailing experience when Rackum asked him, and he stiffly nodded. *With what line of work? The navy?* He nodded again. That's how we came to call him the Admiral. He didn't give Rackum his name when he asked. He only stared at him, deadly, as if daring him to find out what would happen if he prodded further. Rackum nodded in a confused compliance and went to question the other crew members.

We all suspected he was mute like Woody, even though he would mutter a rare swear in moments of frustration every now and again, but we decided to respect his silent nature no matter what the circumstance and tried to assimilate him into the crew as best we could, but none of us had such luck, except for Cathy.

Cathy was a good soul. I don't know how he got roped into this pirating business for someone with such a bright outlook on life as him. When asked about his past, he got grave and quiet, as if a rainy cloud had passed over him, and he would say that he had no desire to speak of it, turn away, and find something else to smile at. That gave me all I needed to know: he wasn't born with an endless love for all things; it was forged in whatever hellfire he was forced to walk through. I think it was because he knew he had to find something to love if he wanted to keep living.

That something to love was the Admiral. When there was nothing to do on the ship, he would sidle up to the Admiral holed up alone in a corner and do whatever he could to crack a smile on the other man's face. I thought it to be a fool's errand, as the Admiral's radiating hostility only reassured me of his wish to be left alone. Cathy either did not see the glaring warning, or he chose not to heed it. I was worried that he might get stabbed if he pestered him too much.

The Admiral did not seem bothered by Cathy's presence, however. He instead seemed amused by Cathy's persistence. He would keep his distance, but his pale eyes would follow Cathy with enraptured attention. Still Cathy could not crack him, but curiously, the Admiral never dissuaded Cathy from trying. On the contrary, he seemed to encourage it, with little acts of kind appreciation as if to say *you will fail, but I appreciate your efforts.*

It was an ordinary day like any other when we were completing our little tasks in preparation and pursuit of our next target when, suddenly, an ugly, horrid noise rang out on the deck. Every head snapped around to its source to find the Admiral, doubled over, clutching his stomach, laughing the most disgusting laugh known to mankind. And there was Cathy steadfast beside him, grinning like a besotted fool, eyes gleaming at the Admiral like he was singing a song more beautiful than any mockingbird could replicate. I think he fell in love with him just then.

They had their matelotage ceremony only a week and a half later. It was a good day. Cathy and the Admiral stood at the bow of the ship, hand-in-hand, pledging before the crew to fight alongside and protect each other in battle and in life, along with the promise to share their assets with one another, a joint-income in life and an inheritance in death. Rackum used his power as a pseudo-captain to bless their union and promise to honor their wishes if either of them should pass.

When they embraced at the end, cheers ruptured among the crew, and rum and wine were passed out in celebration. Through the singing and the laughing and the clinking of glass, I could make out the Admiral and Cathy, still in the same spot as they were at the beginning of the ceremony, in each other's arms, swaying slowly to some secret melody deaf to the rest of us. There were tears in both of their eyes. Cathy held the Admiral's face in his hands, bringing it to his own, and kissed him square on the lips. It was sweet, and I turned away from them with a smile. It seemed wrong to intrude on their private intimacy.

It weighed heavy on my heart, that two people so in love, a love reproached by this accursed society, lay in pain on the grubby floor of a prison, clinging desperately to each other, afraid that if either of them let go, the other would sink into the abyss and never return. They deserved to love free and in laughter, rolling in a field with the sky arched open above them, not here, teetering the edge of survival. I couldn't bear to see their love be crushed under the gravity of their circumstances. And to think, I had a part of it.

"That bullet was meant for me. It should have hit me."

"No one *should* have been shot, Ann," Dobbins responded seriously with an intensity flaring in his eyes. "No one is more worthy of a wound than another; it just happens." Once he felt he got his point across, he decided to let up on the severity and cracked a sly smile. "Besides, you've had your fair share of scars and blood. Leave some of the glory for the rest of us."

This made me scoff. "I don't consider it to be any glory."

Dobbins conceded. "No one really does. We convince ourselves that it is so we can believe our suffering means something."

I nodded. Dobbins did not seem very old to me, but he held a wisdom that could only come from years of experience. Well, at least he had such wisdom when he was sober. The man was notorious among our crew for having the worst impulses once he had drunk more than he had bled. I giggled, thinking of the time we had to talk him out of diving into the choppy waves one night when he was convinced there was a siren singing to him below.

Dobbins raised a brow at me, and I was about to remind him of that memory when a sudden cry startled me from my reverie. It was coming from No Knees Davies.

On the ground, he was writhing on his back to and fro while tears streamed down his face into his scraggly beard. He flopped onto his side and brought his arms to his face to hide from some invisible force of his dreaming mind while his legs were pressed against his chest. Despite being, I'd suppose, in his late fifties, he looked like a babe right there, curled into a nightmare he couldn't control. Memory had that power; it stripped us clean of all the pretenses we built upon our souls and revealed us as the scared, defenseless children we all feared ourselves to be.

"No more!" he yelled against the floor.

While he pleaded with his dreams, a universal groan erupted from the other cells.

"Bloody Christ," Handsome Dick rose out from where he was nestled against Jackie Iron's chest. "Too early for this shit."

"Cease . . . canons, please," Davies still continued. *"No more!* Make it stop."

"I'm up, I'm up!" young Rat Nose squealed, shooting up violently with half-lidded eyes from the cell across from us. He rubbed them and, blinking slowly, he realized where he was and calmed.

"Lord, protect me, *please . . .* "

Dobbins, who was still pressed in some sort

of daze against the iron rails, leapt into action when he recognized the desperation in Davies's voice. He knew exactly what to do; this wasn't the first time we heard the night terrors of No Knees.

While the inmates in his own cell began to rise, Dobbins went to Davies's side and began to shake his shoulder gently while calmly asking "Davies? You have to wake up. It's just a dream, mate."

Davies's eyes flew open, and he pushed Dobbins onto his back and threw his whole body on top of him. Davies reached for his waist's side, where a sword or a pistol would be hung on a belt, but he only clasped air. This proved to be very concerning for him, and he continued to babble under his breath even more, coating Dobbins's face below with flecks of spit. Davies held his empty hands out in front of his face, and his bloodshot eyes grew wider as they jumped from hand to hand, not truly seeing them but fearing them all the same.

Dobbins reached up to pull down Davies's trembling hands and tried again.

"Davies, mate, calm down," he said to him with a steady voice despite the other man's crushing weight and the crazed look that glazed his eyes. "We're just in ol' Spanish-Town Gaol, remember? You're not in the navy, there are no canons, and you're… you're safe."

Davies' shaky breathing leveled out. He removed himself from Dobbins and pressed his eyes closed, trying to block out whatever he believed surrounded him. Dobbins rose and knelt before him, waiting patiently until Davies came to and opened his eyes.

"Thanks, Dobbins. Yer a kind man." Davies sputtered through his large graying beard.

"You good now?"

"Aye, aye, will be in no time," he accompanied this with a false smile, but there was a shakiness to him still.

No Knees Davies. A naval scrimmage many years ago left him without his lower legs, and he was forced to walk around on two crude wooden calves. While the navy let him go, Rackum had seen the natural strength he had in his broad shoulders and veiny arms. He had undeniable upper strength, especially for a man of his age, but while his torso could handle the heavier loads, his legs would easily give out and lose balance. Still, Rackum found a way to work around it and had Seagull, the more wood-savvy member of the crew, create a swing with a pulley system so Davies would be able to pull himself up to the top of the mast with lumber and linen for repairs to the sails.

But now, the English had taken everything from us, including Davies's peg legs. Did he feel any resentment towards any of us? Even though we were all trapped, we at least had the privilege to move and pace and stand as we pleased. While they had stripped us all of our dignity, they stripped him of his personhood. His wooden legs were a part of him, his body, his liberty, and his identity. Hell, it was his name after all: *No Knees Davies.* That's the name he gave us, and that's what we called him.

I wonder, was it even a name he liked, or was it a horrid reminder? I never worked up the courage to ask him.

Each of us had a name like that. We were all called something stupid one day when we left the womb or boarded the deck, by someone else or by ourselves, and that merged with our identity until we could no longer sever our souls from it.

That name, Bonny Ann to John, or *Anne Bonny* to the world, always fell on me like an ill fit cloak, always too big and too heavy for me to feel like it was truly made in my shape. That wasn't who I was. I was simply *myself*, whatever that meant. I felt more akin to the Ann Fulford swaddled in her mother's arms, but I wished I could be the *Ann* reflected in Maura's eyes.

"Apologies, mates," Davies said aloud to us prisoners, but he didn't raise his head to look us in the eye. "Didn' mean to wake ye."

Jackie Iron shuffled away from where he slept next to Handsome Dick, arm and leg sprawled out practically on top of him.

"Yea, and you didn't mean to fire at the English either, I reckon," Handsome Dick muttered, shaking his head.

"I beg yer pardon?" Davies asked.

"Better to beg for forgiveness, No Knees,"

he replied softly, winking at his mate. "Still don't think I'd give it to you."

"I apologized, didn' I? What more can ye take from me?"

"The least you can do, No Knees, is let us get some bloody shuteye," Dick spat out bitterly, propping himself up on his shoulders to glare at the old man.

"Oh, come off it," Davies finally hissed in return, "like we didn' hear Jackie Iron play ye like a bagpipe the other night."

"Ohé!" Jackie lurched up.

Dick pointed a threatening finger at Davies: "You don't get 'bout talk to him like that!"

"Or what? Just leave me 'lone."

"If it wasn't for the bars between us that *you* put us in," Dick rushed to the iron grate that imprisoned him and gripped with white knuckles as he sneered, "I'd kick your bloody arse!"

"He's right," a deep voice echoed from the dark corner behind Dick. There, Rackum sat, shoulders slumped and hair shadowing his face. He titled his head up slightly to shoot daggers at Davies with his brown eyes. "If it wasn't for your reckless shooting, they never would have bothered us."

"That's nae fair," Little Fen spoke up from the cell he shared solely with Rat Nose. Despite his namesake, Fen's large and imposing stature dwarfed the scrawny Rat Nose. "A chance ship half-hid in some cove? The English would've checked us out anyway. They're nosy like tha'."

"And yet," Rackum interrupted, "we'll never know. We could have prepared. We could have quietly escaped. We could have had half a chance before that arsehole fucked it all up."

"Would you stop whining once in your goddamn life," Maura jumped in. I turned behind me to see that she was wide awake now,

"How dare . . . " Rackum sputtered, "I am your *captain*—"

"You see a ship here, Rackum?" She sneered behind her clenched teeth. *"You're* the reason why we're here, pendejo. You, afraid to get your precious frock—your only frock that isn't a shitty, *peasant* cotton—splattered with blood, cowered away while we were all becoming murderers for you. Because we foolishly believed in the freedom you promised us. Alas, you denied it to us because *you* surrendered. We're here in this shitehole because you gave up, you *bitch!*"

"And what would you have me do, huh? Let 'em all kill you, torture you, slowly and painfully, one by one until we were all cut down?"

"I'd rather die fighting on my ship than die hanging for a feckin' audience!"

"Would you all just *shut the fuck up!*"

The entirety of the chamber's inhabitants turned to whoever shouted above them all, and I found that every single one of my crew's eyes rested on me. I stood from where I was sitting and calmly approached the edge of my cell to address everyone as best as I could:

"Shit happens. No one's at fault because no one planned this with intent. Maybe some decisions we didn't know we made led us to this point, but sitting around and pointing fingers at each other isn't going to change anything. Nothing can be changed. What's done is done, and we must accept our fate."

I could look at none of them, so I stared at nothing, focusing my gaze on the creasing shadows of the jilted morning. Yea, in my blank gaze, I found the absence, the abyss, *nothing.* I saw death in this coming shadow.

"We're all going to die," I told them. "We know this. Each and every one of us. And we can't do anything about it. None of this matters."

It was then I found my answer to the question Woody's faith posed: What did I believe in? I believed in *nothing.* The only thing I could be sure of in this life was death, and I knew the reality of the void as intimately as I would have known a scorned lover. And it had finally come to claim its revenge, to claim us all.

"Nothing changes, nothing matters. Don't you get it?" My gaze snapped to Dobbins. "Our trials are in what, Dobbins? Two-three weeks?"

"Just about under a month."

"A month," I laughed in hollow heaves. "Our trials are in a month. Thus marks our judgement, and thus marks our deaths. Yea, a month . . . Heed me now: we *will* be found guilty. We have no defense, no attorney, no witnesses. We will die, so get that through your paper skulls. These petty fights are pointless when the grudges you hoard as rewards will be swiftly returned to their Maker alongside your bodies, but by all means, let their burdening weights sink you into early graves. That choice is yours."

I walked away to the farthest corner, sat on the floor, and blankly stared at my palms lying open on my lap. I didn't dare face any of them. I couldn't.

After some debating silence, I half-heard soft apologies and acceptances until there was nothing but silence and quiet idle chatter.

Something tapped me on the shoulder, and I looked up to see Maura avoiding my eyes with some hesitancy. She spoke up:

"I'm sorry, Ann. I didn't mean to get so riled up and cause you any sort of . . . distress."

"Cause me distress? What about the words you spoke that nearly sent John to an early death?"

Her eyes, pointed fixedly on the floor, widened with guilt. "*Och*, d'ya want me to apologize to him?"

I shrugged. "Not unless you feel you need to."

"It's not him I'm worried about, Ann," she chuckled and shook her head before finally meeting my stare.

I rolled my eyes, saying, "Don't be. It's pointless. Did you not listen to what I said?"

"It's no burden to worry about you, Ann. On the contrary, I consider it a great honor."

Saying that, she puffed out her chest, mocking the English soldiers we've seen, and knocking her right fist over her heart. I could not stifle a laugh, and Maura merely grinned, having accomplished what she had set out to do.

But dread still gnawed at my bones like a starving bitch, hungry for hope that was simply not there. The stoniness of my heart must have made its way to my sullen face for Maura grasped my shoulders with an anchoring comfort.

"My dear Ann, you must know how much you mean to me."

I smiled sadly. "If we were not here, I would say you were my dearest friend."

"Why not say it here?"

I opened my mouth to respond, but my throat ran dry as my words ran away.

Maura must have taken pity on my wavering state as she simply clicked her tongue and enveloped me into a deep embrace, sliding her arms around my neck. We had never touched each other like this before—it was always a casual clap on the back, the nudge of an elbow, the brushing of hands—so it took me a few moments to catch up with her, but I eventually wrapped my awkward arms around her in turn.

"I understand you, Ann," Maura said into my shoulder. "You needn't speak and explain."

But did she understand me? I couldn't even

understand myself, and so how could I claim this Ann she believed she saw? That version of me was a shadow, a figment that has no shape nor voice. Staring aimlessly past the slope of Maura's shoulder, I only found the same empty shadows of the cells, but the skin on my arms erupted into gooseflesh with the creeping feeling I was being watched.

There were eyes in the abyss. Those eyes, duller than slate, the lifeless hazel-gray of my own, saw my soul and knew the words to every part of myself I couldn't name, didn't *want* to name. I buried myself further into Maura, hiding from their damning stare in the crook of her neck. Yet, the more I clung to Maura, the further the shadows crept closer. I had to push her away, I had to flee from their—*my own*—violating gaze, but how could I leave? In the warmth of her collarbone, I found respite. Her cool hands grazed my neck, and I could breathe. Our hearts met the other's pace when we held each other close. She was a shelter for a woman—a girl—a *ghost*—unsure of her fear, unsure if she was more afraid of the darkness, of death, or of herself.

But I couldn't stay, and neither could she.

I broke away from our embrace. I held Maura by her shoulders at arm's length while I looked around. The shadows had receded, but they had not disappeared. They merely lingered in the corners, between the bricks, under the furrowed brows of our disheartened comrades. I hesitantly turned back to Maura and finally met her gaze. In her eyes where her bountiful energy usually resided, a new, weary disappointment had replaced it.

I wondered what she saw when she looked into mine.

Maura eventually broke the hush that settled over us with some uncertainty:

"What do we do now?"

I sighed. It was the question that plagued all of us, the one we tried to answer with stories or fidgeting or fighting, hoping to fill up the dreaded space that spanned the seemingly endless amount of time between now and whenever *then* would be. My thumbs instinctually rubbed small circles onto Maura's shoulders, hoping to be reassuring, and said the only thing I could think of:

"Now, Maura, we wait."

CHAPTER 3:

Hung on Gibbits in Chains

WAITING PROVED DIFFICULT. IT WAS STICKY AND SLOW, and every day passed in boredom, in nothing. I had grown increasingly restless. My hands were dry and cracked from the breezeless air, and the skin frayed out like fishing nets around my fingernails. Dirt caked at the seam where skin met nail, so I dug at them. They had grown significantly, and I thought, how long have I been here?

I never stayed so long in one place. We were always on the move, me and my mum. Someone was always after us, and there was always something new right around the corner. At least, that's what my mum thought. She was a hopeful sod—despite a no good husband abandoning her, despite having to solely provide for a child's hungry mouth, despite being subjected to the horrors of poverty and crime. Perhaps that's why she had hope; without hope, she had no reason to keep moving.

It was hard to keep moving in prison. Thankfully, my wound had mostly healed, and I took that opportunity to pace around my cell, to pick at the mortar in between the aging bricks, to unravel the splitting strings on my sweat-stained tunic. I couldn't sit still. Sitting still reminded me of where I was, where I wasn't. The feeling falling from my legs, my arms, the immobility creeping up my body like a poison numbing me. The silence was deafening, but the little sounds, close and far away, were too quiet. There was nothing, but that nothing was everywhere; in my lungs, in my nose, in my hollow heart. My heart was hollow! It was a shell, a heavy shell, beating blood in waves through my hands and my feet until that beating consumed me that soon I couldn't hear it, couldn't feel it. *Is this what death was like?* The feeling of being trapped in your body slowly wasting away, leaving you with nothing to do, no one to be, nowhere to *hide?*

"Are you all right, Ann?"

Maura's voice cut through my spiraling thoughts, and she sidled up to me, her brows pinched with worry, and eyes wide with care as she searched my face for an answer. I looked down at my bleeding hand.

I picked the fingernail too hard. I had torn off half of my nail on my left hand's ring finger, but it still hung on to my remaining nail, stuck up like a ragged banner. I couldn't leave it like that, so I braced myself and tore it free. I winced, failing to stifle a grunt.

"Here," Maura said and tore a scrap from her soft shirt. It was Maura's favorite tunic—one that she had before I had known her—because of its color. It was a pale green, but I could tell by the lines about the wrinkles and edges that it must have once been the color of fresh summer leaves before the sun had dulled it. Now faded, filthy, and forgotten, it ripped easily, and she tied the scrap around my bloody finger.

"It wasn't that serious," I murmured into my chest.

"Doesn't matter," she replied, finishing the knot. I watched as the red slowly bled into the green fabric, making a muddied brown.

"Thanks," I said softly, refusing to look at Maura's face.

"So," she put a comforting hand on my knee, "want-a tell me what that was about?"

My eyes darted up to Maura's. They were narrow and incredibly dark, framed by long soft eyelashes. It was like peering into the sea at night and getting lost in lazy crescent waves. At times, the pale daylight beyond the bars illuminated the depths of her ocean—revealing a wine-deep brown. That color was intoxicating. Perhaps I was selfish to believe that light only shined for me. If eyes are the windows to the soul, as I've heard it said, then Maura's eyes were the morning sunlight. That glow was stronger than any fist, knocking at the thick glassy pane of my own eye, pleading for me to draw back the curtains and let her flood my room with light, to warm my own soul.

But those eyes would lose their own light in a few weeks, maybe even a few days. And I would watch it happen. *Would I see her hang first, I wondered, and watch her eyes bulge out of their sockets, waiting in agony for her neck to snap? Or would* she *witness my body jerk uncontrollably in the air as the noose crushed my throat? Would the last fading thing I see be the terror on her face, slack and screaming? Or, perhaps, our executioners would be so kind as to let us hang together, swaying side by side.*

No, I didn't want to let her in, not when I was about to lose her so soon.

I closed the curtains behind my eyes.

"No," I told her sheepishly. "I don't."

Maura leaned back and removed her hand from my knee, looking away. "Suit yourself," was all she said. She slumped against the wall again and closed her eyes, resuming her nap, but I doubted her ability to fall asleep so quickly. She probably just didn't want to look at me anymore.

I leaned back on the wall and my shoulders sagged against the cool brick. It snagged on my brown cotton coat, one of the only things the guards had let me keep. Our sword belts and guns were stashed somewhere along with Woody's cameo and Davies's legs, I presumed, but they could've disposed of them easily. They could have been floating in the Caribbean's endless waves for all I knew.

They took Maura's hat. It was a black beaver skin—one with a large brim, a buckle, and a monstrous peacock feather—and it fluttered in the salty sea breeze. It suited her short brown hair that sprayed out like curly ribbons beneath it. I wished they had let her keep it.

I wondered why they hadn't given Maura and me an apron or a bonnet to 'properly' dress ourselves up in. Perhaps they were too scared to go near us. Perhaps they wanted to make an example out of us.

Maura and I were not opposed to feminine fashion. We delighted in adorning ourselves with fancy dresses stolen from passing merchants, as did the rest of the crew. We would sometimes aid Cathy, Dick, and Dobbins in cinching up stays, pulling bodices over their heads, or styling obnoxious powdered wigs for them so they could perform for the crew in song and dance. However, the heavy layers were never the most practical, so Maura and I donned tunics and sloppes most of the time on deck.

It was hard to keep those stories alive, as if it was sacrilegious to think of such bright, lighthearted memories in such a dark and dismal place. Perhaps we were cocky, perhaps we were criminals. We wanted to dance in the waves and sing to the songs of sirens. Now, we had to pay the players.

I am not here to condone our actions, only to recount their consequences. And, believe me, we would not have chosen the life of piracy out of our own free will. Most of us wanted to escape. Most of us wanted to run away. If a life of blood and brine attracted wretched souls like us, what does that say of the lives we left behind?

And yet, who will read this? Who will believe us and see us as equals, as human beings?

We were mourning our own deaths, since no one else would. We would never receive proper funerals. There'd be few visitors anyhow, little in the name of loved ones to lean on our shallow graves and weep for our early departures.

If we had happy homes, we would not be so quick to abandon them.

Little Fen was one of the few who had a happy childhood. Happy enough, at least, to fill the lonely time we had together with stories of his youth. He was a large man, tall, with muscle and fat insulating his entire body from the cool touch of our stone prison. His shoulder-length hair was mostly gray; I believed it came on prematurely, for he was young with compassion and hearty laughs. He was a good-natured sort of fellow, but one was not to mess with him, lest they were willing to risk a broken nose.

He was in the midst of recounting the light thievery he dabbled in his youth. I watched Rat Nose cross his legs beside Little Fen, and Jackie

Iron leaned on the iron bars between their cells, each listening with an eager intent.

" . . . an' there, Anthony came up to me wit' a horse—don't ask me where he got the damn horse because I couldn' tell ye—and grabbed me by me arm and sat me behind 'im, an' we rode 'way."

Little laughs began to bubble up from Fen's mouth, and he had to pause his history to catch his breath before he continued.

"We lost few candlesticks 'long the way, but who knew me knight in shinin' armor would be me *brother!*"

Laughter erupted from the three of them, but the loudest came from Little Fen who laughed with his whole belly, and leaning forward, it shook the rest of his body. It was a complete and whole sound compared to Jackie's wheezing and Rat Nose's high-pitched, nasally outbursts.

"Me mum was furious when we came home," chuckled Little Fen, "'cause we were all dirty, sticks in our hair an' bugs in our eyes, an' now we 'ad a horse ta feed! But she soon quieted once she saw the silver we brought home."

"Did ya Pa whip ya when ya got home?" Rat Nose piped up. He was sixteen or seventeen years at best, naive and corny-faced. Even though his body was thin and gangly, he was far from the starving kid Little Fen introduced to Rackam those few months ago. He was more than willing to earn his keep, an eagerness that can only be attributed to youth, but that badgering became irritating at times, and he lacked the insight to know when to stop. His nose was pointed like a skyward mast, tugging on his upper lip so that he constantly bore his gums and crooked teeth to the world. They stuck out even more when he looked up at Little Fen.

Little Fen's mouth tightened when he debated on what to tell the kid. "Me father died when I was jus' a wee babe. He was so bloody drunk one night that he stumbled off a dock and drowned in the sea. Me mum an' me brothers had to tend the farm ourselves after tha'."

"Oh," Rat Nose remarked, lips pursed in deep consideration. "Did ya Ma whip ya?"

"She pulled us by the ear sometimes, an' maybe smacked the back of our heads, but tha' was it. She didnae like handlin' us like tha'."

"Oh," Rat Nose mumbled again, head drooping down.

"Why d'ye ask?"

"Well," Rat Nose stared at the ground, brows furrowed together like a pair of furry caterpillars. "My Pa beat us. My brother, sister, and me. Mostly me. A lot. It would be a shoe, or sometimes he'd throw the plates, or just use his hands. I thought . . . I thought that happened to everybody. And when he kicked me out . . . "

"Why did he kick you out?" Jackie Iron spoke up, his English very punctual and meticulous.

"Uh," Rat Nose was never good at finding his words, but luckily the men around him were patient. "I lost my job. It was a small thing at the mill, and the master got mad at me when I spilled grain all over the floor for—" he gulped and hunched his shoulders "-for the third time that month. They were really heavy . . . Anyway, it was just my sister and me who worked then. She had a sewing thing with some other ladies in town, and there was me and the mill, but my brother was sick in bed with the pox, and my Pa . . . well, he had been out of a job for some months, doing odd ones at the docks. So, we really needed the money. Really badly. And I . . . "

Rat Nose somehow managed to make himself smaller as he shrank on the floor.

"I messed up. Pa, he got me, and my nose broke and my left eye went all black and blue. And then, he threw me out. Told me, 'don't ya ever bring ya sorry motha-f-fucking face back here, Thomas. Ya . . . Ya not my son.'"

Rat Nose brought his knees to his chest, sobbing slightly when he clutched them.

"Didn't even get my things, didn't even get to say goodbye. But I deserved it! I know I did. That's why he did it. Because I was bad. I was a bad son, yea?"

"No." This time, Dobbins, uninvited, spoke out from the other side of the room where he sat with Woody. He spoke with a soft tone that masked the stench of anger that reeked, "your *Pa* was just that bad of a father."

Rat Nose's eyes lurched up at these words,

and he stared at Dobbins, conflicting emotion running along the undercurrent of his mind.

"I-I . . . " he mumbled at first before growing louder with accusation. "Don't speak about my Pa like that! You didn't know my Pa. *Don't* know him. Pa was, well, he was not a perfect man—none of us are—but he was my Pa. I loved him, and he loved me!"

"Easy now, boy," Jackie Iron reasoned as he reached a careful hand through the bars to place it on the boy's shoulder. Rat Nose swatted the hand away and shuffled back like he was caught in a trap.

"He-he was a good man. Ya don't know him like I do. He was looking out for the family, looking out for me and Martha and Billy, and he just did what he had to do."

"He didn't have to hurt you, toss you out like rubbish," Dobbins argued.

"Yes, he did!" Rat Nose intensely rattled on. "I was bad. I failed him. It's my fault, ya hear? It's *my fault!*"

The tears broke on his lowered eyelids, and he wiped them away furiously, hoping no one would see, but all eyes were on him now. However, none had held the same rage as Dobbins, and he soon voiced it:

"It's not your fault. You are not to blame."

"Quit being dense, Dobbins," Rat Nose shot back.

"You quit being dense and *listen to me!*"

Dobbins pressed himself to the gate, and the bars rattled when he grabbed them. "It's not your fault! He should not have kicked you out. That is such a- a vile thing to do, and to your own child—"

"How the hell would ya know, huh? Ya not my Pa."

Dobbins shrunk away from that jab and looked down at his open palms that lay on his lap.

"No, I'm not. But I was someone else's."

A hush went over all of us who leaned in to listen.

"A boy back in Philly," Dobbins interrupted the silence. When I looked at him, his sandy blond hair shrouded his eyes. "Daniel. That's his name. Or . . . was. He was a cute little fella. He had his mother's blue eyes and my father's black hair. Couldn't stop smiling. He had a dimple on his left cheek when he smiled, not his right. Only his left. I dunno who he got that from."

He chuckled sadly to himself.

"He was a wild kid. He loved to climb trees and run around in the streets, but good God, he would always fall, always scrape himself up. Alice, my, uh, wife would always have to clean him up, every day it seemed, but he never stopped smiling. He wanted to do everything, to be everything. And I let him be because he was so damn happy."

His face soon darkened from where it lit up in memory of his son.

"But there was an accident. I didn't see what had happened, but a mate of his rushed me one day to the marketplace, and there he lay . . . on the ground . . . his belly bleeding out, mangled like . . . tattered red ribbons . . . "

He sniffed and wiped his leaking nose.

"It was some coach that got him. Maybe he spooked the horses, or got too close to those goddamned landowning topping men, but . . . he was gone. He died soon after we found him. I can only hope the Lord spared him of my own sins and led him to the pearly gates . . . oh, who am I fooling!"

A pitying smile appeared over his red face as he curled up in on himself. Woody reached to place his hand on top of Dobbins's shaking shoulders, but Dobbins shrugged him off, still having more to say:

"Alice blamed me. I mean, I guess she was right. Told me I should have never encouraged him, should have stopped him, should have . . . She told me to piss off, leave, and that I did. I hopped on the first merchant boat to the Caribbean, and the last I heard of her, she told everyone she knew that I had died. She's probably remarried by now, I'm sure of it. I hope she is. Forgotten all about me, probably, forgotten . . . "

He shook his head and mustered as much strength as he could to press his message home.

"Danny, my poor boy, was the best thing that ever happened to me. He was everything to me, and I would give anything, do *anything* for him. I'd kill and die and kill again if it meant I could see my little boy once more. My poor boy . . . So, forgive me, Rat Nose, for saying this, but your father is the Devil's kin for abusing the greatest thing God could ever give a man. He was my light and my joy, you understand? Your father was a right bastard for turning that away, when I would do anything, he was my little boy . . . "

I heard the choked noises that came from Dobbins once he succumbed to his grief. He buried his head in his hands and leaned forward, trembling but now quiet. Woody took this as an opening to place a hand on his back to rub small circles. Cathy, who had retreated into the arms of his lover, knowing his touch to the grieving man was unwanted, gave the Admiral a look of unspoken sympathy and helplessness. While the latter didn't move, his eyes fell upon Dobbins with a pitying yet protective look. No Knees was the one in their cell whose eyes shook with a frantic memory I could not place, and it left him uncertain of what to do with himself, so he just stayed where he was.

"But, my Pa," Rat Nose said, throwing his voice into the air to no one in particular, maybe to no one at all. "He loves-loved me, he has to . . . "

"I dinnae, son, I dinnae," Little Fen huffed sadly as he wrapped around the boy's shoulders. "Maybe he did, but not in the way he should've."

Rat Nose quickly turned his head to Little Fen, face red and contorted with confusion, denial, and grief. Little Fen still had more to say to Rat

Nose:

"S' not yer fault, Thomas. Ye didn' deserve tha', ye don't. Yer a good boy. Ye jus' got a . . . a shite dad."

Finally giving into the weight of his emotions, Rat Nose began to cry, throwing his arms around Little Fen and burying his face in his chest. Little Fen, surprised but welcoming, furrowed his brows with newfound tenderness as he held the boy close to him, rocking him back and forth as he sobbed.

"S' all right, son," he whispered into his oily hair. "S' all right, now. I've got ye. Yer safe."

Oh, we would never be safe, we all knew that, and the despaired look in Little Fen's eyes told me that he had not forgotten that, but he still squeezed the boy tighter on the prison floor, hoping to make the lie he told true, even if for a moment.

There was only silence save for the sobs muffled by Little Fen's large chest. Jackie Iron drew back his hand in the grate to give them both space, but Handsome Dick, beside him, took it, intertwining their fingers. The two looked at each other with an understanding I could not comprehend.

Rackum lay behind them, body curled towards the wall. He wanted to look like he was sleeping, but I knew better. John was so helpless in times like these, and I would say he was scared of these moments, of what it meant for himself. He never wanted to be seen as vulnerable or weak, but in avoiding these feelings, it made him look even more the coward. At least it did to me.

Seagull's reaction was what troubled me. He just sat there beside our once-captain, awake yet motionless. As his eyes were downcast to the floor, a dark shadow passed over his face. I could not discern the feelings fleeting across his face.

I did not know much about Seagull. He kept to himself, if he was not keeping to John. He was his first mate, but I suspected that his duties to his captain extended more than that. He often visited the captain's private quarters at night, but they would be distant or bickering the next day. It was either all honey or all turd with them.

He wasn't a secretive man, but he wasn't a public one either. He simply minded his own business, but there was something about the way he bowed his head—in shame, in anger, in fear, I did not know—that made me believe that he was fleeing from something—perhaps something within himself—and it was catching up.

Yet, all of us were pursued by a devil in some way, one born from ourselves, one we ran from tirelessly since the day we could walk.

And now, there was nowhere to run. We were trapped, cornered, and caught, and that was it. We would soon be shuffled to the bar where our skins would be auctioned off.

I could feel my own devil, breathing the faint breeze of salt and rotted fish down my neck as I looked at all the people I should have called friends and was too afraid to call family.

I cared for them. And I could not keep them. My devil was making sure of it. That is what terrified me.

❄ ❄ ❄

I WAS ALONE ON THE BEACH THIS TIME. *I sat on the island's edge, the clear Caribbean Ocean stretching out before me, with a bottle of wine in my hand. I took a drink, but the wine turned to water in my mouth, then to ash. I spat it out. The ashes were my mother's, I was sure of it, but they disappeared into the sand. I dug through the white grains, trying to retrieve them while tears dripped from my eyes. I struck something solid and cold, and I uncovered it some more until my treasure lay out before me: a skeleton trapped in a gibbet, an iron cage made to suspend a corpse into the air for all to see and fear. The gibbet was rusty and old, but the skeleton was not fully decomposed. There was skin and flesh still peeling off the bones. Were they my mother's bones? Were they mine? But it was a green shirt and a beaver-skin hat that clad the skeleton. The skeleton belonged to another. Maura's brown eyes were set in the skull, but one rolled back into the darkness beyond the bone facade. I tried to scream out, but only smoke emerged from my mouth. Smoke. My heart was burning inside.*

I awoke with a shout, startling Maura who slept beside me. Her hand shot out from her side to shield my body as she abruptly sat up. Her hair, still short but now shiny and full of grease, flapped around her head as she instinctually looked around for the source of danger. I sat up and tentatively placed a hand on her shoulder. She flinched, but soon settled.

"I'm sorry, Maura," I quietly said to her. "I'm all right. I just . . . had a bad dream."

She turned to look at me, and her reddened eyes looked as tired as mine felt. Perhaps we each were having bad dreams at that time. It did not surprise me.

"You don't have to rise to protect me, Maura," I gravely teased her. "I can handle my own."

"I know, Ann," she whispered, lingering sleep still straining her voice. "Believe me, I know, but you shouldn't have to."

"But I have to. Both of us do."

"Aye, that we do. I s'pose it's a habit of mine."

"What, protecting me?"

"Just protecting . . . " Maura trailed away, unsure of what words to use. "Well, my father was a sailor, so it was just me, my mam, my sisters and brothers for most of it. My mam tried to find work wherever she could for some little coin, and I was the oldest, so it fell on me to look out for everyone else. S'pose it's natural to protect my . . . family."

Her eyes finally looked to mine sheepishly, unguarded but uncertain of what she might find.

I wanted to smile and reciprocate; I wanted to say the thing I knew to be true, *You're my family, too*, but something held me back.

The vision of Maura's rotting skeleton in gibbets and chains came to my mind, how I cried and screamed and wanted to bury it in the sand again so I wouldn't see it, and maybe the desperate loss that lodged itself in my throat would be swallowed and digested. *Just* maybe, the smoke that billowed out my mouth in ashy coughs would clear if I quelled the anguished fire that burned inside me whenever I looked at Maura.

How could I have a *family* now knowing it'd be ripped from my hands later? No, the burden of insurmountable loss was impossible for me to bear. I just couldn't.

So, I did nothing. I weakly nodded and fiddled with the strings that threaded the dip of my chemise, tightening it across my bosom, as if locking my heart deep inside my chest. I never felt more like a coward in my entire life.

The sound of rattling metal made every head turn towards the large wooden door, forever locked save for the meals and drink. It swung open on its iron hinges, and two soldiers of red uniforms walked through in synchronous motion, placing themselves on either side of the open door.

Then, a man of stout stature walked through; the stiff powdered curls that framed his face bounced in rhythm as he walked into our quarters with light steps, trying to prevent the dirty floor from touching his shiny, buckled black shoes. Those who were sleeping still were then roused by their inmates in his presence.

He opened the leather-bound book he clutched in his hands and spoke in a posh accent:

"On Wednesday, the sixteenth day of November, in the seventh year of the reign of our sovereign Lord George, by the Grace of God, of Britain, France and Ireland, King, and of Jamaica, Lord, Defender of the Faith, etcetera. His said Majesty King George calls upon the prisoners tried for piracies, felonies, and robberies committed upon the high seas to be brought to the Court of the town of Saint Jago de la Vega." He looked up from the paper and set his eyes upon the prisoners in front of him for the first time. "When your name is spoken, please announce your presence.

"John Rackam: late of the island of Providence in America; Mariner; late Commander of a certain pirate sloop of an unknown name."

Rackum waved an unenthusiastic hand in the air.

"George Fetherstone: late of said island of Providence; Mariner; late Master of said sloop."

Seagull looked at the man gravely and nodded in his direction.

"Richard Corner: late of said island of

Providence; Mariner; late Quarter Master of said sloop."

"Right here," Handsome Dick drolly replied. "Not bloody going anywhere," he muttered under his breath before adding a belated "sir" at the end for good measure.

"John Davies, John Howell, Patrick Carty, Thomas Earl, and Noah Harwood: late also of the said island of Providence; Mariners . . . "

No Knees, Jackie Iron, Cathy, the Admiral, and Woody each raised their hands, respectively.

"And James Dobbin, late of the town of Philadelphia, in the province of Pennsylvania; Mariner."

"Aye, sir," Dobbins sighed with defeat. "We're all here."

"Right, all part of said sloop's Crew," the man continued with a disgusted snarl. "Under the jurisdiction of this Court, you will be taken to the Bar before the Court, where you will be tried by Sir Nicholas Lawes, Captain General and Governor-in-Chief, named and appointed by His Majesty's Commission for the trying of Pirates, and the esquires members of our Council of our said island of Jamaica for your crimes against the Crown. Men—" he motioned with a pristine finger to the soldiers behind him, "—unlock the cells, tie our prisoners, and bring them to the Court. The rest of you will remain until your own trials have commenced."

The first two cells were emptied out and the

men were prepared with rope around their wrists, save for No Knees who was hoisted by several men into a chair with wheels on its sides and pushed out of his cell before the rest. Little Fen, Rat Nose, Maura, and I, left untouched in our cells, looked at each other, attempting to silently communicate our confusion and fear. Soon, those being tried were all tied to one another by one rope before being led by the soldiers through the door. The squeak and thud of the door closing behind them left trails of deafening echoes amid the vacancy of the cells.

Despite the emptiness of the room, it felt even more suffocating than it did with the nine other bodies crowded into it. I became more aware of the walls, the thick air, and the dust that danced in the air without a care in the world.

Bile rose in my throat, clawing like a frightened liquid beast begging to be released from its cage, but I forced it back down into my gut. The sour taste remained, a bitter reminder; I would have to ignore it.

I heard distant voices, sobs even, but I ignored them too. I couldn't bear it, the weight of our fates looming like smoke in the air, choking our lungs. *Perhaps if I ignore it,* I reasoned, *I will not feel the fire burning me.*

I turned towards the wall and laid myself down, bringing my knees to my chest, white knuckles and blue veins popping from the hands that clung to them. I wanted to bring every bit of myself to my chest, praying for sleep to take me away from this prison floor and the body that threatened to flood itself with tears.

* * *

I DRIFTED IN AND OUT OF A LIGHT SLEEP LIKE A BATTERED DINGHY being pulled back and forth by the tide. It was restless and uncomfortable, but I had no strength to move myself.

I faced the stones in the wall, scarce ants crawling this way and that on the stones' ridges. I envied them. I envied everything that moved with ease.

But they were not free, were they? They were at the mercy of men who could easily end their lives with a press of a thumb and a forefinger. They scurried into invisible holes between the mortar when I waved a hand near them. I grinned ever so slightly. They ran like I once did, but they could not escape. I found a straggler and pushed it against the wall with my finger, rolling the sticky insect guts that were left on my fingertips into a ball and flicking it away. *Stupid buggers,* I thought, frowning.

I closed my eyes once more, but threads

of conversation found their way to my ears. I recognized Little Fen's thick, husky voice:

" . . . was the runt o' the litter. I could barely come to the waist o' me mum, so they called me Little Fen. Names stick, e'en when ye grow into a princod twice the size of those who named ye." I heard him chuckle. "Wha' 'bout 'Maura'?"

"It's Irish," Maura added.

"Ha! I ken tha' y'were by the way ye talk," Little Fen remarked, pleased with himself, "but ye nae from the isles, or ye'd be a Broganeer. Yer somethin' else."

"Isn't that just Mary?" Rat Nose suddenly accused. There was no malice he directed at Maura. Rat Nose just wasn't at the age where he knew to withhold his own suspicion.

Lying with my back toward them, I could still perfectly picture the way Maura must have shrugged, raising her eyebrows, lips pressed tight in mischief. It was a move she pulled too often on me when she teased.

"Maura comes from Mary, but I am Maura, not *just Mary*, Rat Nose. There are enough Mary's in the world, little Virgin Mothers running households and watching their sons become what they could never dream of being themselves. I won't disappear into the lot of them."

The day Maura and I had first met was the day Rackum had gathered a group of people in Nassau. That New Providence was a lawless land before my time with a government bribed and laid claim over by English privateers. It became a sort of republic for pirates, that is, until that crooked Woodes Rogers came in as governor to clean up the place.

There were those of us who were still determined. After my mother was taken away, I made my way there to try my hand at thievery, careful to avoid the fate of many desperate port-women. I had heard of John Rackam when he turned himself in to Rogers, and he was given a royal pardon and even a commission from the governor. Everyone thought he was a traitor, sucking up to the English, but his time as a good man lasted less than a year once rumors went around that he was making a new crew.

I met him as did other men at Herm's Tavern where piss may have tasted better than the beer they served. He liked my gumption and my wit, so I was welcomed on the crew. While he moved on to other candidates, I deigned to avoid them, so I sat alone in the snug of the pub, nursing a pint. But a shadow passed over me, one with a flowing coat and a floppy hat. She asked to buy me the next round, so I obliged.

We had two more pints that night while Rackum was a few tables over interviewing the rest of our future crew, and I liked her instantly. She struck up a conversation with me, asking me strangely about my life and my dreams. She was bold, impish even, but buried underneath her sharp tongue, there was an overflowing well of curiosity. Each person was a tapestry to her, a complete picture but fraying at the edges, and she longed to pull at the threads until it all unraveled and she could truly see what founded a person from a pile of tangled string. It was heady to be the object of her study, even if only for a night. She found out why I left the Bahamas, I found out her name was Maura Reed.

What she told Rat Nose reminded me of that first conversation, when I had asked her why she fell into piracy in the first place. I will forever remember the answer she gave me and the way my admiration for the woman increased tenfold that night:

"To make a name for myself, I reckon. I want to be more than the lass on the shore."

The memory of that made me smile, even on the dank and dirty ground. I drifted back to a dreamless sea once more.

* * *

I WAS JOLTED OUT OF MY SLEEP TO THE SOUND of quiet sobs. They were too high and choppy to be anyone else's but Rat Nose's. They sounded painful and constricted in his throat, but at least he was fortunate enough to be accompanied by the soft hushes of Little Fen.

I turned my head slightly and saw the two of them, alone in their cell. No one had returned from the hearing yet, and Maura was dozing away in a corner, so it was just Rat Nose wrapped in Little Fen's arms as he wept into his large shoulder. I turned back to the wall to give the two privacy.

"I j-just . . . " Rat Nose stuttered in between harsh breaths, "Pa didn't l-love me. Bet B-Billy and Martha didn't. Did anyone? *Jesus-Mary-and-Joseph,* I'm gonna die without anyone loving me . . . "

"Settle down now, son, it'll be all right," Little Fen, but even without looking at him, I could hear the worry wavering in his voice. "Y'are loved, loved by all of us. At least by me, I know tha' for sure."

Little Fen chuckled at that one, hoping to breathe some levity into the air, but Rat Nose made no indication that he felt it. Little Fen tried again:

"How 'bout this: for . . . for as long as we have, I'll be yer Pa, and I'll love ye like a Pa should. How 'bout tha'?"

Rat Nose quieted for a moment, in shock presumably, before bursting out, crying once more. It was more muffled than it was before; he was hugging Little Fen as hard as he could, I was sure of it.

Little Fen was always looking out for Rat Nose, guiding the young boy into the ways of sailing and piracy. Little Fen, from my conversations, had seen firsthand the brutality of life at sea. Maybe he wanted to spare Rat Nose from all of that, as much as he can.

"Th-thank you," Rat Nose whispered, but I heard it.

"Of course, m'boy," Little Fen replied with solemn foreboding, but his voice was unmistakably full of love. "Of course," he repeated, and they didn't speak after that.

It felt imposing to keep an ear out anyway, so I slept again.

* * *

MAURA HAD A MOLE ABOVE HER LIP. It was a small dark thing that twitched when her lips curled in concentration. Some people said it was the mark of the devil, but some French nobles would cover their faces with moleskin replicas. I wasn't sure what to make of it; it was neither beautiful nor ugly, it was a bump of skin on her face. But it was on Maura's face, so some part of me was fascinated with it.

It bobbed up and down while she picked at the peeling mortar on our cell's wall. She had been going at it for a few minutes now, ever since I had woken up. She didn't notice me stir, so I was just content to watch her lazily from the floor.

"Trying to escape, are we?" I teased, smiling at my friend.

I had startled her out of whatever daze she had been lulled to, and her head snapped towards me in an instant.

"No, sorry, I just," she began, fumbling with her words. "It's been some few hours, I reckon, since they left. I don't know . . . I'm just nervous is all. Can't sit still."

"I know that feeling," I sympathized. "I can feel my heart rattling in my ribs every second more I stay here—*we* stay here. I think it's trying to leave me."

"Truly?" She abandoned the wall, no longer interested, and focused her attention on me. "You're remarkable at hiding it. You appear so calm."

I laugh at that notion. "That's because I keep it all inside me, Maura. It's all buzzing in here—" I gesture vaguely towards my bosom with my hands "—like bees in a hive, but its entrance has been sealed. Nowhere to go, nowhere to be but here. So I sit. And I wait. And I think. What more can I do?"

"What do you think of?"

I thought of a squat, little palm tree by the sea that I used to climb as a girl, pretending to be a queen. I thought of the mackerel pie my mum used to make for the men that visited our room. I thought of the shadows that crept through the windows on the night my mother was taken away. I thought of the stinking sloop I slept in for a fortnight on my way to Nassau. I thought of Rackum's gold tooth glinting in the candlelit pub. I thought of the white foam that used to caress our ship's sides as we cut through the blue sea. I thought of nights under the open stars, swinging in a cool hammock, while whispering secrets to a friend, to Maura. I thought of Maura's soft giggle that she'd try to hide behind the back of her hand. Of the wee curls that licked the back of her exposed neck. Of her mole . . . I thought of Maura a lot.

But I told something different, but something nevertheless still true.

"The Green Flash. I mull it over in my head, over and over again, like a waterwheel; one image being scooped up, making its run along the wheel, before being dumped into another. I bounce between many ideas of what it might have been, my only source coming from the legends passed down to me."

"How do you picture it?"

Maura leaned into my space, eyes glistening with curiosity and lips quirked up in amusement, tugging on that damned little mole. It was awfully distracting, so I closed my eyes to imagine the green scene and describe to Maura what I saw beneath my eyelids:

"The sun sinks below the water, and from there, green fire sparks to life on the horizon as flame does to rum. From there, I see shades of sailors past emerging from its center, swimming through the air like a school of sickly, pale green fish. They are wailing with jaws unhinged, but the distance makes it sound only like a melancholy hum. They scatter across the sky, souls finally released from the sea. They are free to find the ones they loved. But all this happens within a moment, and I blink, and it ends, and the remaining souls are sucked back into the watery depths from whence their drowned bodies once sank."

I opened my eyes once my vision ended, and I found Maura, face mere inches from mine. Her soft, warm breath breezed by my cheek, and her eyes peered up to me with what I hoped was wonder. Suddenly, she laughed and leaned back.

"Blood and 'ounds, Bonny Ann! Perhaps there's some guts in your brains after all. A shame the poetry gets buried under all the swears you keep on your tongue!"

"Oh, mock me not!" I laughed along and pushed her away gently. "Let me keep my dreams."

"Aye, I shan't take them from you, however fantastical they may be. Even without a sword, I've seen your fangs."

"Fantastical? Ha! Unlike you, I only have fantasies to base them off of."

I paused and remembered the prank Maura pulled on me on our last day on the sea, and I was overcome with the urge to know.

"When the Green Flash happened and you saw it, was it something like that? Did you feel it? Was my dream close?" And within a moment, my mind cleared at once. I halted my speech before

Maura could answer, reeling in my eagerness and shaking my head. "No, no, don't tell me. Not now, anyway. I'll only be saddened. I've made my own memories of it, and I like them as they are."

I grinned at her, and she grinned back, and it was as if some secret was being shared between us, only for us, even if I did not know what language our mind spoke.

Our moment was abruptly interrupted by the click-clacking of awkward keys in heavy iron locks, signaling our friends' awaited arrival. Maura and I straightened ourselves in anticipation.

The same guard that brought them out led them in, and everyone else followed silently behind them. Woody was the first in line with his head hanging low, his mop of brown curls obscuring his eyes, but beneath it all, I saw his bottom lip jutting out slightly. He looked up when he stepped across the threshold, and he met my anxious eyes. He simply frowned and shook his head. There was nothing more to say, and that was all I needed to know.

The rest of our once crew piled through and the guards attended to their binds. Rackum was the one to take up the rear. His expression was blank and tired, the kind of look one has when exiting the tavern in the morn after a night-long bar fight. I thought that he wanted to appear stoic, but I realized then that I did not know what he wanted anymore.

I wasn't sure if I ever knew what he wanted.

Everyone knew the same short set of facts about him: he was once part of Captain Charles Vane's crew on his *Ranger* brigantine; he staged a coup against Vane after he branded his captain a coward for not attacking a French man-o-war; he conquered many a vessel for his own privateer army, losing and regaining them in stride before ultimately forfeiting it all in favor of a quiet, virtuous life; then, just as quickly, he forfeited *that* life and returned to the sea.

I had called this man a friend before because when he wasn't a captain, he was fairly pleasant company—save for when he tried to make a mistress of me. But when I saw him sullenly shuffle into his cell with hands unbound and aim his persistent glower at the ground, I realized then that I pitied him more than I respected him.

The guards left and locked the doors behind them, and we all sat uncomfortably with one another in our cells again, not knowing what to say. We, who were patiently waiting for the better hours of the day, gazed upon those who had just entered, but they pointedly avoided our eyes, staring at the ground beneath them. Little Fen cleared his throat and was the first to breach the silence:

"How did it go?"

Dobbins sighed, about to answer, but Rackum beat him to it:

"We were all unanimously found guilty by the court for 'piracy, robbery, and felony.'" He uselessly wetted his chapped lips with a dry tongue and spoke with a steady voice. "We are sentenced to death by hanging."

This was never a surprise to any of us, but the absolute inevitability lingering in his words hit the four of us who lagged behind like a battering ram.

"Is that what you pleaded? Guilty?" I asked him myself.

"'Course not. That'd be foolish."

"Foolish, yea?" Maura piped up. "Blood and 'ounds, Rackum, sometimes I think you're just a blustering, stiff-rump *eejit*, but then you pull this shite and make me wonder if you have even an ounce of respect for any of us. Now, I know you're just some stiff-rump who's been fed with a fire shovel to piss more than you feckin' drink."

"I'd like to see you at the bar, with a hundred eyes upon your face and back, staying true to the crimes pinned against you," he shot back with a devious snarl, "but I'm afraid, *Mad Mary*, I'll be dead by then."

His lips curled around the nickname, once given out of reverence for her ferocity, but now hissed between his yellowed teeth, it had become an accusation. Maura breathed in deeply to prepare a defense against his vicious seething.

"You were a coward, John."

It wasn't Maura that spoke; the voice came from Seagull—John's own first mate who trailed after him with every order, who never breathed a word against his captain. Except now, looking like *God's revenge against murder.*

"Fucking—pardon, Seagull?" Rackum demanded. His face boiled red with blood as he turned towards the man standing beside him.

"Spare me your shit. You babbled like a babe in front of 'em, claiming that you *'only attacked the Spanish,'* when our prosecutors even had that bastard Spenlow, as English as King George's drawers—whom we *stole* sot-weed and those bags of pimento, mind you—at the damn stand against us. We held him hostage for two days, for Christ's sake, and you have the gall to deny all of it? If you were going to plead innocence, then you could have at least held your forked tongue. Whose side were you even on? *Are* on, dammit! We didn't need your bullshit excuses, and they shan't hear your begging. *Ha!* Some fucking show you put on—you really became a panting spaniel out there, doing tricks for the court. You couldn't even let the rest of us stand on our own trial with dignity. You made us all fucking fools out there."

Rackum's jaw clenched, teeth grinding painfully on each other in a way that I swore could be heard across the room. He stood up to meet Seagull, to challenge him with his towering height while he worked up a response, but Seagull ranted on:

"We all knew we were going to fucking die—Hell, I didn't expect to last this long! So why'd you have to put your foot in your mouth—"

"I did what I had to do—"

"To 'protect your crew,' John? Or to protect yourself? Kissing those fuckers' feet for some scraps of respect before you're dead as a nit. No, you don't care about us; you only care about yourself! You want to be like one of 'em!" He snarled with disgust. "Yea, a free man with power in his hand and coin in his purse to do whatever he damn pleases! Not some poor, wretched sailor; not some husband playing House. You couldn't even bear the mundanity of your wife and children after you traded in your pennon flag, because you were *nobody*. Not *the* Captain John Rackam, but a *Hanktelo*, wise as Waltham's calf, who swallows a hare every night. So, you abandoned that life just as quickly as you are denying this one because you're afraid, John. Afraid of disappearing, of being *humiliated*, but above all, you're afraid of being at the mercy of another. You just have to have it all, don't ya? In any way you can get it, no matter who you use, who you fuck over."

Rackum pulled back his fist and chalked Seagull in the face, breaking his nose and splattering blood across the wall behind him. Seagull, bringing a careful finger to his nose and touching the blood that oozed from it, soon returned the favor by striking a blow in Rackum's gut, making him bend over, but Rackum refused to fall.

"You don't know shit about me, George!" he hissed through his teeth, clutching his middle.

"I know too much, John. When Vane was a lily-livered belly-gut, who was the first to vote for you? I sailed the Ranger, the Kingston, and all the shitholes in between for you. I left my girl in Nassau for you. She's carrying my babe, Johnny!"

"I didn't ask you to do any of that."

"No, you didn't," Seagull bowed his head with a sad smile. "I reckon I'm just eating my nails believing that my sacrifices are worth something to you."

"Worth?" Rackum growled back at him. "I don't owe you a damn thing!"

"Perhaps not," said Seagull emboldened, looking John dead in the eyes, "but as your pintle-merchant, I expect at least half a crown."

Rackum was the first to strike, lunging at Seagull and pinning him to the ground. He threw his fists, punching his jaw and his shoulder until Seagull kneed him in the crotch, creating an opening to blacken his eye. Jackie Iron and Handsome Dick, who had both been sitting on the sidelines waiting for the scene to simmer down, finally pulled the two apart. While Rackum struggled in Handsome Dick's grasp, Seagull only bared his teeth; a smile or a grimace, I couldn't say. He spat a bloody wad onto his captain's feet and said:

"*You fucking cunt!* I gave my life for you! After everything we've been through, how dare you deny it before all those wankers!"

Rackum yelled back at him, words lost in

jumbled fury, before Handsome Dick shook him and held him back.

"Hang your arse, Rackum," he whispered in his ear. "If the guards hear, they'll be on us in a minute to thrash us all."

Rackum noticeably calmed down, but he shook off Dick's hands and paced around the small confines of the cell, running bloodied fingers through his greasy hair. Jackie's grip on Seagull's shoulders morphed into a protective stance, but I couldn't tell if he was trying to protect Rackum or Seagull himself.

"Now, listen here," Handsome Dick commanded with eyes alight with fiery frustration. "You may be entitled to some fucking *lovers' quarrel* or whatever the hell this is, but you two are not the only ones here who are going to die with regrets in a few days' time."

"It's none of your business," said Rackum.

"Rackum, would you just shut the fuck up and fucking put your arse to anchor! It is everyone's business when we're stuck here together. You don't get privacy in prison. We don't want to listen to you dashers bickering about who did what or who loved who."

Seagull quickly interjected: "I never said I loved him."

"And I never said *who*," Handsome Dick shot right back. "Figure your shit out or die in deadly suspense. *Hang together, or hang alone.* Not my fucking problem. Just leave me and Jackie the fuck *out of it."*

Dick resigned himself to the corner he and Jackie Iron usually occupied. Jackie met him there, sitting beside him. Dick scratched a scab that grew on his knee, something he had a recent nervous habit of doing ever since he earned it in our little skirmish with the English. If Jackie Iron wasn't there to take his hands whenever he did it and thread his fingers through his own, as he did in that moment, it probably would burst open and never close.

When they looked at each other, it was like two souls through a looking glass, one on either side. I assure you, neither looked anything like the other. Handsome Dick was a pasty Englishman through and through, and his skin only gained its living color from the sun's brutality whereas Jackie Iron had a rich brown complexion, a glimpse of his parents, kidnapped from Africa and enslaved. Jackie's hair was short and wiry, with a few hairs curling on his chin, while Dick's was outgrown to his shoulders. Jackie Iron had a French flair to his English that sounded like an egg had lodged itself in his throat, and Dick's voice gave the impression that he never stepped foot out of England. They would never be mistaken for the other in a million years, and yet, when they looked at each other, they held some sort of sparkling recognition in their eyes, as if finally laying eyes on the missing half of their body.

They were tethered together long before

joining Rackum's crew. Handsome Dick had a small schooner in New Providence at the time Rackum was rounding up a crew, and he gave Dick a hefty sum to have both the boat and Dick as its quartermaster, but Dick wouldn't budge unless Rackum agreed to take on his matelot, Jackie Iron, as well.

They were a force to be reckoned with on deck. They fought side by side, moving and switching blades as if their swords were dually wielded by the same person.

However coordinated they were, they were not always the brightest. Jackie had a little more common sense than Dick, and there were many times when Jackie had to restrain him, but both would egg each other on and unconditionally go along with each other's plans.

When we had taken two Frenchmen for prisoners after a passionate fight, we threw them in the cargo hold, tied back-to-back. Dick circled them like a shark stalking prey. Despite his shorter stature, his words evoked a cowering, exaggerated terror in the French. After he had his share, Jackie Iron went up to them and spoke something in his native French before walking away from them, leaving them pale with real fear. I had asked Jackie about this after, and he merely laughed, saying that those Frenchmen didn't know a lick of English. He instructed the hostages beforehand to nod and act scared of whatever Dick said to them (unless they wanted to lose their fingers to his wooden teeth).

Along with our foes, Rackum proved no match for the two of them either. Dick—distractedly blabbering among the crew with his big mouth—once dropped a crate of plundered gunpowder as he was handing it off to Maura below deck. Black sand spilled all over the planks, so Rackum grabbed him by his collar and yelled nothing but spit into his face. It was Jackie Iron who so 'gently' reminded him of whose ship they were on, who was squatting on it, and who therefore could dirty it as much as he damn pleased. (This was all said with a sharpened dagger to his throat, of course.) Rackum yielded, and he had Rat Nose and Woody clean up the mess.

As Jackie went around doing his chores for the day with a smirk and a smug air, Dick watched him with adoring eyes like he had painted the stars in the sky in a swoon-worthy declaration of love.

None of us crewmates could understand them, why they unconditionally supported each other in their adventures and their mishaps, what drew one to the other or made them protect each other as viciously as they did, but I suppose we didn't need to. They knew each other truly, seeing through their skin and flesh to the very light of their soul and the shadow of their sin, and spoke words of love in their own spiritual tongue. They didn't have to prove anything to anyone, least of all to us, of their love and the lengths that they would go for each other.

But, even still, when Jackie Iron had cupped Dick's face in his hands and kissed him soundly in the gray light of prison, leaving Dick with a soft tender smile blooming on his face, I was convinced enough.

Seagull buried his bloodied face away, but Rackum, like me, was captivated with the couple's kiss. Although, he did not look at them with the same admiration I did. He looked on with a hostile hunger, and I wondered for a moment if John was jealous of them.

I turned away, and my eyes instinctually landed on Maura's form, huddled against the bars as she chatted mindlessly with Cathy as the Admiral observed. She held her knees to her chest as she listened intently to Cathy, laughing here or commenting there when it was appropriate. Her teeth, though not white, glistened like pearls against her pink mouth when her lips curled in a smile.

I thought of Andrew, the sailor she shared her shiners and her blankets with. I felt an ache, like my heart was being grated against my ribs, but it was unclear what for: the fact that Maura was abandoned by the man she might have loved, or the fact that she might have loved him at all.

I didn't know what to do with that new and sudden pain, so I promptly ignored it and leaned back against the wall with my clasped hands cushioning my head. I idly listened to their conspiring voices: Cathy's soft, timid, exuberant conversation compared to Maura's, which was shrewd, jaunty, and utterly irresistible.

* * *

WHEN NIGHT FELL LIKE A FUNERAL SHROUD and light was smothered to sleep, so were we. One by one, we drifted away into the moonless darkness, and I listened to their soft breaths filling the air. John Rackum was notorious for, as Dobbins called it, "driving his hogs to the market" in the night, but tonight he was remarkably quiet. They were all remarkably quiet. Soon enough, their breathing faded away into the background of my mind until there was nothing left at all.

Nothing. The silence should have lulled me into a peaceful slumber like it did with everyone else, but after growing used to the rhythms of my crew during the past few months, it only put me off-kilter. *Nothing.* Like they were all dead, like all their souls had abandoned their bodies and were ferried to another world and I was left alone among their corpses strewn across the floor. *Nothing.* The nothingness stretched out before me, and where the ceiling once was, there seemed to only be a pool of darkness above me, ever-expanding into eternity. *Nothing.* I lost the feeling in my body as I floated upwards into the inky expanse. *Nothing.* It was all-consuming, that *nothing*, and it filled my lungs and peeled back the flesh of my eyes until I had no eyes at all (but did I ever need them, when there was only *nothing* to see?).

This must be death, I thought. I was not confident in Heaven, I was not afraid of Hell, but I was afraid of this, of being pressed under a weightless black sludge, of being rendered immovable and at the mercy of an empty void, of being trapped with only myself and the darkness, of *nothing*.

"George?"

A faint sound brought me back to my body, and I once again felt the cold stone beneath me, saw the dirty ceiling above me, and heard John's whispering rasp.

"What is it?" I heard Seagull dully respond. I dared not to move and make my presence known to them.

"I . . . I don't know what to say."

"Then let me sleep, John."

"No, I . . . " Rackum's voice died away in his throat, and, sighing, he tried once more:

"I never loved you, George. And I . . . regret if I had ever made you believe that."

There was a long stretch of silence, but it wasn't painful in the way it was before. It was only the silence that came when everything must be said, but it was impossible to settle on how.

"I don't think I ever wanted you to, Johnny," Seagull said at long last. "Love me, that is. Hell, I don't really believe I loved you either. I just wanted you in some way. Your body? Yea, the nights we drunkenly fell into bed together gave me some sort of warmth I craved. But, most of all, I think, I wanted your attention, your approval. But I never really wanted your heart, Johnny. And I didn't really want you to have mine."

"Saving that for the gal back home?"

Seagull paused, contemplating. "No. Not really. Fidelity, that's her name. Ironic, innit? Considering she's a Piper's wife, just at the punch-house around the corner from the postmaster in Providence. Jesus, you may have even tasted her before. Anyhow, she fancied me a bit too strongly. She was fun, but I didn't want to marry old boots . . . "

My intestines squirmed at that moment, hearing at how he so easily dismissed that poor girl. It brought back images of my mother, who was a *Drury Lane Vestal* like Fidelity. But my mum's name was Alice. When it was just the two of us, I called her Mamma, and she'd call me *dove*. She had long, blond hair that she piled on top of her head, but I loved those little hairs that fell around her face, and I loved them even more when she twirled them absent-mindedly around her ears. She told me that I got my red hair from my father, and that she should have taken that as a warning against him. Red hair was the mark of the devil, after all, and he was far from a saint. Yet, she promised to love me as best as she could despite my devil-kissed locks.

Seagull's solemness broke through those painful memories:

" . . . but it was too late. She got preg-a-nant. Not much I could do but, well, promise to marry her. We didn't have money for it officially, but the bann was good enough. It was sickening, Johnny, the way she dangled on me, but it was done. I told myself that it was my duty as a man. But then you came back. You promised me a new life of freedom, an escape. We were low on money anyhow, so I followed you . . . Oh, the dam of that is a whisker, Johnny. Even if she were the richest heiress in the Bahamas, I'd have still followed you, even to Cipangu . . . "

Over the years of plotting and swearing and crying, I gathered that I was born of some man who promised to love my mother, to take her away from that horrid life filled with the men she submitted her body to out of desperation. He vowed to make his fortune on the seas and return to herself and the son she promised to bear. Alas, he never came back, and she got stuck with a daughter named Ann. I guess they both broke their promises.

"It was never your fault," Seagull continued. "It was mine. It's easier to blame you than admit I was . . . I am just a louse. And now I'll die and she'll be left alone with a wee babe with none providing for her, thinking her scoundrel husband ditched her for good. Well, wouldn't be too far off, I reckon ... "

We lived in a little room that my mother rented from the Abbess of the brothel, but I only slept there on Sundays and Thursdays. Most nights, she'd send me off into the alley behind the house. A little overhang was set up there for me with straw bedding and a ratty blanket. The place was secluded, so I never felt in danger, save for that one time a dog had found its way there. I climbed onto the brothel's roof that night to escape. The dog barked the entire night before stalking away, but at least the stars above me were lovely.

The day, however, we'd spend in each other's company. Once a month we'd visit the bakery for fresh bread just for us, but we'd mostly stay in our little chamber. She'd sew up the holes in my only two dresses, my Sunday dress which I rarely wore (we rarely went) and the little plain frock I'd run around in. But what I remember most is the wistful way she stared out the window, suddenly whipping her bonnet-clad head around at every horse's hoof clomping by or the rapping of shoes on cobblestone, like she was always expecting someone's company.

One fateful night, one of the ladies found me in the corner of the alley and brought me into the house. I found my mum lying in bed, without blood or expression in her face. I thought she was dead, but no, the woman told me—aye, Annabel was her name—that *she had suffered a fit of hysteria while tending to a patron. Don't worry. She'll get back on her feet soon enough.*

She did get back on her feet, but her feet wanted to take her far away. She rounded up our things in a tattered leather-bound chest, and whatever didn't fit, she told me to leave behind. *Even if he is looking,* she muttered to herself while packing away her only fine dress, *if for some goddamn reason he's looking, I don't want him to find me. Find us,* she added hastily and turned to me with bloodshot eyes. *If he ever lays a hand on you, Ann, I'll kill him . . . I'll kill him, Ann . . .*

My mother knew what it was to be that *whore* Seagull left behind, and I might as well have been the newborn he never met. We women were the sacrifices for men's greedy fires, becoming the ghosts that haunted our own lives.

I knew their story too well, for I had lived it. The ink of that forgotten tale ran through my veins, words encased in my paper-pale skin.

But he would never know that. He would be dead before he had the chance to see the consequences, and still, I don't think he would return to that woman and child even if he could.

Bastard, I wanted to shout, but I kept silent. His choices were his own, but that did not mean I couldn't resent him for them. How fortunate for him, to be a man who could fuck off as he pleased without a care for the women he left in the wake behind him.

But look where that got him. In prison mere days before his hanging, confessing to an estranged man in the dark. Now, on his deathbed, he finally had the balls to feel remorse?

And still, I kept silent. This had nothing to do with me, no matter how much I convinced myself it did. It was between him and John, who likewise could think of nothing to say in response, so Seagull spoke up for him to fill the silence:

"Don't the two of us make a pair, Johnny. Two lonely souls wandering the midnight, already dead to the lives we left behind, and lost on this plane until we go up the ladder to bed."

John still kept his trap shut. The only sounds came from the murmuring Caribbean breeze, softly scraping the bricks like lips brushing the skin of a lover, but it did not soothe the discomfort radiating between the two across the cell.

"What was her name?" Seagull cautiously asked, trying to sound disinterested despite his burning curiosity. "Your wife?"

Rackum gave no reply to his question, only curtly and coldly addressing Seagull like he would to any crewmate:

"That'll be all, Seagull. Get some shuteye."

Besides the soft rustle of cloth, I heard no sound again that night until Rackum's snores inevitably erupted and echoed across the walls.

I pitied John. So very afraid to be seen beyond his fragile shell of masculinity and rationality. Even when someone got close enough to see through his disguise and offer an oriental lily of sympathy, hoping to relieve him from the burden of imprisoning his heart in his chest, he turned him away.

He always kept his cards close to his chest. I remember a rare moment when it was just the two of us. He was as drunk as Davy's sow. He let slip something about a wife or a lover or a child or whatnot. I prodded for just a little more, but he closed up like a bitter clam and miraculously regained sobriety. He bid me goodnight and swiftly stood up to leave.

I never learned what John's personal life was, and he never offered it. To the rest of the crew, it seemed that he was too proud to let them in, that they weren't worthy of his heart while the rest of them were spilling their guts. But could it have been the shame of his mistakes that made him retain his secrecy? Did he desperately want to forget it, amputate it from his personage? Or was it special to him? Did he, deep inside, revere his family, and did they respect him? Did he want to hoard the memory of them for the ones who would understand, far from the reach of those who would misinterpret it and plague it with their own perspectives?

No matter, I thought. He chose his fate, and he would live with it until he could no longer. Rackum wanted to let that memory die with him. And so it did.

❉ ❉ ❉

R AT NOSE AND LITTLE FEN WERE TAKEN THE NEXT DAY. It was the same procedure as the day before with the rest of the crew; the same man with the curls came in with the guards and called for Thomas Brown and John Fenwick respectfully, the two having committed some other acts of joint piracy before being admitted into Rackum's crew that had to be additionally tried for.

Rat Nose's knees shook violently before being shooed through the door, but Little Fen kindly placed a large, soothing hand on the boy's back and said some quiet, gentle words to him. The heavy door slammed before the image of them smiling nervously at each other, and we were left in the silence again.

The rest of the day was wasted away in anxious apprehension. The trial only prolonged the inevitable, we knew this, but our hearts didn't, and they were still beating away in our chests as if we weren't waiting for the verdict on our friends' necks. Nothing from our minds could ease the tension that flooded our bodies.

The rays of sun had only moved a little

across the walls when Little Fen and Rat Nose eventually returned. Rat Nose entered the room crying, his eyes red and his thin, pointed lips glossed with the snot that trickled from his nose. Little Fen was more collected for Rat Nose's sake, but I still saw how his lower eyelids still cupped tears that were begging to be shed.

After they had been settled and were soon left alone again, Little Fen took the lithe Rat Nose in his arms. He rocked him gently but uncertainly, like a newfound father would an infant, while the boy cried. They needed not tell us what had come of the trial for we all knew. And if we didn't beforehand, their despair said all we needed to know.

I was compelled to look away, refusing to intrude on the intimacy of their shared grief. As I did, I caught Maura's eyes. They were tinged pink around their rims, glossed with water, and they seemed to well a little more once trapped in my gaze.

She looked wretched, and my heart screamed to touch her, to comfort her. I held out a hand and brushed away a short lock of hair that clung to her sweaty temples, and then I found her hand to squeeze. She unfolded her hand and interlocked her fingers with mine before smiling defeatedly at me.

I had nothing to say. All the words that passed through my mind got snagged on the thorns of emotion that lined my throat.

* * *

"ENOUGH OF THIS DAMNED GLOOM," Handsome Dick pierced the silence with his booming voice and the clanging lead tray that he threw to the ground. The guards had delivered what would be for some of us our last meal. Each of us had a lobster, poor enough to feed prisons and still plentiful enough to pile up a couple feet along the shore. It was bland and chewy, having been mass-boiled over a large fire, and we tore at their shells like animals.

"*Râlala, Dick,* watch where you throw that shit?" Jackie Iron said through a mouthful of hardtack, pulling up his legs from where the food splattered on the floor.

"No!" Dick replied. "If this is to be our Last Supper, then let us break bread and get drunk on this piss-poor beer as if it were the finest wine!"

"Have you no respect?" Seagull asked him incredulously.

"None, in fact," Dick chuckled. "If I were to die, I would go to the pub, announce it to everyone that I was dying, and declare that the drinks were on me. Then, I'd drink and sing with friends and strangers alike until my heart stops and my body drops. Can't settle the tab if you're stuck in Davy Jones's locker!"

He roared with laughter, and many of us could not help but laugh with them.

"Pray, raise your glass," continued Dick, raising his crude cup, a far cry from any fine crystal. "To the end. Yes, it may be grim and sad, but it is an end of a good life, I must say. The best I could have done with my lot, at least."

It didn't matter how true his words were, beforehand or afterwards. We believed them to be true at that moment. We had to, or else we would all begin to sob. We all gathered to the edge of cells to raise our cups in unison.

"And ends must be celebrated to remember what we had lived before, to remember what we lived *for*. May history remember us, or forget us all. Either way, we'll know what's true."

Aye's and *here, here's* and a spare, soft *huzzah from the Admiral* bounced across the walls, but I could not find it within myself to say anything.

"May we drink tonight to die tomorrow. Cheers!"

"To your health," I heard Dobbins cheer, which Little Fen echoed across the room. When No Knees meekly said it back to him, Dobbins just laughed and knocked their cups together. Woody wordlessly jammed his own cup between the other two's with a large smile at the end.

"Santé!" Jackie said, downing his glass, before taking Dick's face in his hands and pulling him into a deep kiss.

"Sláinte," a voice beside me said, a voice laced with affection and a twinge of remorse. It was, of course, belonging to Maura.

Health, we all cried in a language that belonged to ourselves. Health evoked the future and a tomorrow full of safety and prosperity, and we had to wish for one another while parting, as if ensuring that we will be whole the next time we meet, as if we will find our way back to each other.

But looking into Maura's endless eyes, I could not help but fall into the fantasy that this story is not done yet. *Our* story. I smiled at the thought.

"Sláinte," I parroted back at her with some delicate hesitancy. But still, we reveled in the shared tongue, foreign yet intimate, passed down from our far-away mothers. They must now rot in a ditch somewhere, forgotten, but we remembered that word they gave us. Hell, it was the only word my mother gave me, the only word she understood and could remember from distant memories of family gatherings, back when everyone was alive and willing to drink with us. When she passed it onto me, it came with a deluded sense of belonging to something I couldn't understand. At least it was enough to understand Maura and to know I belonged beside her. We knocked our cups together, spilling our liquid into each other's, and we smiled while drinking, no matter how repulsive the beer was.

The chatter that had emerged among our party had begun to die down as Dick's cup had clattered across the rails, getting everyone's attention as he stood up. He began to sing an English tune I was unfamiliar with:

"Here's a health to the King and a lasting peace,
To faction an end, to wealth increase;
Come, let us drink it while we have breath,
For there's no drinking after death,
And he that will this health deny,
Down among the dead men,
Down among the dead men,
Down, down, down, down,
Down among the dead men let him lie!"

Those who knew the last words of the chorus joined in, and sang along with Handsome Dick:

"Let charming Beauty's health go round,
In whom celestial joys are found;
And may confusion still pursue,
The senseless woman hating crew,
And they that woman's health deny . . . "

My stare fell upon Woody who was nodding along to the music, at least able to feel the rhythm, the noise, and the celebration of his companions even without sound.

"Down among the dead men,
Down among the dead men,
Down, down, down, down,
Down among the dead men let him lie!"

Maura had picked up on the chorus' pattern

and joined along, with a vigor and ferocity I had not seen since the day we had been captured. I wanted to sing too, if not for the song then for the spirit that had passed through my bones at the sight of Maura. Yet, I refrained. There was an anchor weighing down my own spirit still.

> *"May love and wine their joys maintain,*
> *And their united pleasures reign;*
> *While smiling plenty crowns the land,*
> *We'll sing the joys that both afford:*
> *And they that won't with us comply . . . "*

They sang into the night until their voices grew hoarse and rasp, but I had not joined them once. Every ounce of their spirit was poured into their song, as if relinquishing their souls to the air before they could be trapped inside the bodies that were soon to be broken by the rope of a noose. I could not find it within myself to enjoy the evening, knowing that they'd leave me behind and take their melodies with them.

Their voices live on in my memory as their hearts do not:

> *"Down among the dead men . . . "*

Rackum, Seagull, Handsome Dick, Jackie Iron, No Knees Davies, were taken away the next morning on Friday the eighteenth day of November, 1720, to be hung in Gallows-Point, Port Royal until their necks snapped. The bodies of the first three were strewn across Jamaica: Rackum to Plumb-point, Seagull to Bush-Key, Dick to Gun-Key; their bodies were displayed in gibbets as a *"publick example."* I do not know where the rest of their corpses were taken. Would the souls of Handsome Dick and Jackie Iron, the revolving lovers, be able to find one another if their mortal vessels could not lie side by side?

"Down among the dead men . . . "

The morning after, Saturday, the nineteenth of November, 1720, Woody, Dobbins, Cathy, and the Admiral were executed in Kingston. Cathy and the Admiral were the last to leave the cell. They walked out, hand in hand, and heads held high. They smiled at each other one last time before the door was closed behind them forever.

"Down!"

Executions were postponed on Sunday, *a day of rest*, but they once again came to claim Rat Nose and Little Fen on the following Monday, the twenty-first of November, 1720. They hung together as father and son in Port Royal at the same Gallows-point.

"Down!"

My only comfort was that my friends, my companions, and my crew did not die alone.

"Down!"

And I, too, would hang in Maura's company, but that did not comfort me.

"Down!

I would lose her to the darkness that consumed everyone before, and then I would truly be alone.

"Down among the dead men . . . "

There would be no love in death. Only *nothing.*

"Let him lie!"

CHAPTER 4:

By the Largeness of Their Breasts

A WEEK HAD PASSED; I COUNTED THE TIMES THE SUN ROSE and fell across the cell. It was the only thing that distracted me from my thoughts, the only light that saved me from the pooling darkness.

It was so quiet, so empty. There was once warmth in these cells, I had to remind myself. It was filled with laughter and song, but it was taken away along with the people I dared to call my own. Now, I couldn't even find the feeling within myself to acknowledge the cold.

There were living, breathing people here once, people I touched and held and danced with, and now they were gone. I couldn't understand that someone could be just *gone,* just like that. I had seen people die under my nose, on the sea or on the streets, but I had always turned away from them before I could tempt death to follow me next. But now, the people I was once close with were far away and never to return. I did not see the life leave their eyes nor the air be squeezed from their throats. Was that better or worse, I wondered? In my heart, I could still foolishly feel their presence. My heart lied to me, but what else could it do? People don't die to the heart. When everyone is dead and you are alone, it still continues to beat with the tender fullness of friendship. Those ties cannot be severed, only weakened with time, even if there is no longer anyone to tie my heart *to*. It just beats on falsely and aimlessly towards nothing. *That* is what was painful.

My mind, on the other hand, couldn't grapple with the reality of death, that a life would exist until it simply didn't. It almost split itself in half trying to.

It was difficult to cry, I found. I had never been very weepy, even as a little girl. My mum didn't like it when I cried. She would tell me that I didn't have anything to cry about, that we'd leave and it wouldn't even matter. *Why waste your tears?* My mother would ask. *We'll be gone soon.*

Whenever my feelings became too loud, I would simply fly away—that's how I thought of it. Instincts would possess me and sever my soul from my body, and floating above me, it would observe the place where my body hunched over itself on the blasted prison floor; I'd see my eyes stare ahead of me, wide and dry.

Then Maura would come into the frame. She'd reach a hand out and pull my arm from where it would be squeezed around my tummy. She'd be gentle, always, as she slowly would take my palm and press it to her own chest. I'd feel her heart beat, *bump, ba-dump, bump, ba-dump*. There was something alive under my hand, something that pulsed in waves of blood and expanded with breath, and I was not as alone as I had once thought. My soul would return to my body to greet whoever this angel with the feather-light touch was.

And it was always Maura. I'd find my eyes again and see out of them, and there would be her face, calmly peering at mine. Her wavy locks that curled around her face, her deep brown eyes shining with unshed tears, her mole above her thin lips, all of it, and it gave its undivided attention to me, as if I was the most beautiful thing in the world, something worthy of a heated gaze like that. It melted the numbing ice that encroached upon me, and I would feel the heat that blossomed underneath my hand.

Then, once knowing I had returned to my senses, Maura would let her eyelids droop, her long dark lashes grazing her cheeks like the kiss of a butterfly's wing, and she would inhale deeply through her nose, exaggerating it to the point where I could hear it all around me. She'd breathe out through her mouth and repeat this motion, inviting me to join her. So I did. I matched her rhythm, followed her pace, and soon, the only thing on my mind was her face, her breath, and my hand resting over her heart. The death and loss that once loomed in my thoughts were gone, and it was Maura. It was always Maura.

We were all that was left, her and me. I thought that, maybe, I could be happy, just the two of us.

But I was confusing thoughts with dreams.

❋ ❋ ❋

I AM SICK OF DREAMING! NO MORE DREAMS, *I screamed across the docks, but no sound emerged. This mattered not to me. I was late to the lighthouse. I lived in a lighthouse with a girl named Maura. I had to bring her the dead hen for supper; it hung across my neck on a rope. I walked across the planks and they made a plunking sound. Plunk, plunk, plunk, I said back to them. That meant 'good morning,' but that made no sense because it was evening. I pressed on. I had to get home. There was a monk seal on the docks. It tipped its hat to me, what a gentleman. My feet found dirt, and the dirt found grass, and the grass found flowers, and soon enough, I was home! The door was opened and a soft, warm yellow light shone from inside, and Maura was there to greet me in the doorway! I smiled at her. I walked up to her and grabbed her face with my hands and kissed her on the lips. But there were eyes in the windows. Then everything fell away into darkness, and I sunk into the darkness, and there was nothing but the darkness, and—oh, God. That's all there ever was.*

I awoke, and I was crying. I had not cried since the night my mum was arrested.

Maura was already awake, sitting by the bars, and she rushed to my side in moments.

"What, Ann, what is it?" She questioned me, eyes darting all around my face for anything that could tell her what I could not bring myself to say.

"A bad dream? Was it a bad dream?" she asked again.

No, I thought. *It was good. It was nice. It was home.* But I stayed silent.

"Hush now," she shushed me before wrapping me in her arms and bringing my head to her chest. She hooked her chin over my head, and I could feel the rumble in her bosom when she spoke, "it wasn't real, Ann. You're still right here. It wasn't real."

This only made me cry even harder.

I clutched her shirt, and she pressed me to her body even more.

What am I doing in her arms? A voice wormed inside of me. *I can't make home here. I have to go, I have to leave before it's gone. I don't want to cry over this again. I can't cry. Mamma wouldn't like it.*

I snapped into my senses, and I promptly pried myself from Maura's pull and pushed her away from me. Her back hit the floor, and she stared up at me with bewildered, wide eyes.

I stuttered nonsensically, unsure of what I should say and afraid of what I wanted to.

My frail attempts were cut short by the loud shoves of the door being unlocked.

Two officers whom I didn't recognize walked in and stood by either side of the door. Their military training and steadfast focus were broken by my quick, heavy breaths, and they both turned to look at me.

"They're blubbering again," one said quietly, rolling his eyes.

"Is this one with hysteria? Is she fit for trial?" The other commented as that same short, well-dressed man with the powdered wig walked in. He was the one who always came to collect us for their trials.

"It does not matter. She will be taken to the bar either way, lest you forget she is still a traitor to the Crown despite her sex."

I retreated into myself at the sound of their comments, bringing my shoulders to my ears and hiding my face away. On the sea, sailing far away from this dreaded society where we women were reduced to our sex and how well our bodies presented it, I had almost forgotten the leering looks men gave as they looked down on someone such as myself, cut down to simply some*thing.* A disgrace to my feminine nature. I wiped my stinging eyes with my wrist, hoping to press the tears back into my sockets. It didn't work.

The man began to read off his book:

"On Monday, the twenty eighth day of November, in the seventh year of the reign of our sovereign Lord George, by the Grace of God, of Britain, France and Ireland, King, and of Jamaica, Lord, Defender of the Faith, etcetera. His said Majesty King George calls upon the prisoners, *Mary Read* and *Anne Bonny,* tried for piracies, felonies, and robberies committed upon the high seas to be brought to the Court of the town of Saint Jago de la Vega." He paused his reading and looked up from his note. "And which of you is Anne, and which of you is Mary?"

Neither of us spoke, as those were not our names.

"Come, speak up now! We haven't all day."

Prompted by his words, one of the guards banged on the bars with the butt of his musket, shaking us out of our daze. Maura stammered out:

"I-I am . . . Mary. And this is Anne." At the sound of my name, she pointed to me, but the man only looked back at his paper.

"Under the jurisdiction of this Court, you will be taken to the Bar before the Court, where you will be tried by Sir Nicholas Lawes, Captain General and Governor-in-Chief, named and appointed by His Majesty's Commission for the trying of Pirates, and the esquires members of our Council of our said island of Jamaica for your crimes against the Crown. Unlock the ladies," he said to the guards, "bind them, and lead them to the courtroom."

The other keys rattled against the metal in sharp, clanging sounds as the first guard unlocked our cell. They leaned down to where we were on the floor to tie us with rope at our wrists before hoisting us up at our feet and pushing us through the gate. The bookkeeper led us through the door from the room.

We followed him along a dark hallway while the two guards, at our heels behind us, cradled their guns in their right arm at all times. We passed by many other doors, all secured by heavy wooden bars, bolts, and locks that peeled with rust caused by the humidity. There was no sunlight to be seen, only candles mounted to the stone walls.

"Why did he call me Anne Bonny?" I finally asked Maura the question on my mind, careful to keep my voice at a whisper.

"That is what they know you as," she earnestly replied, leaning into my space. "Bonny Ann, Anne Bonny. They must have heard it from some witness to one of our raids. We did like to throw it around. Well, Rackum at least did . . . "

Rackum's face swam into my mind. He was unshaven and dirty the last I saw of him, and I couldn't tell where the grime ended and the beard began.

That Friday when he was being rounded up with the rest of them to be wed to the noose, he rushed to my cell and clung to the bars. They were trying to pry him away, but he gripped the metal until his knuckles turned white, exposing bone, all the while pleading to me for a farewell kiss.

I held no adoration for that man in my heart, and after everything we had been through, even the faint feelings of friendship slowly began to sour. But something in my heart clenched when I saw how pathetic he was there: an unrecognizable, desperate man, begging for one last sweet grace. Perhaps I could have denied Captain John Rackam, but that hollow man before me had no name, and I could not deny a blameless stranger his last request. So, I leaned forward through the bars and pecked him quickly on his chapped, bleeding lips. When I pulled away, he was knocked on the head by a soldier, falling limp into his arms. He was dragged out of there, partially unconscious, but the stupid, sloppy grin that lingered on his face was John's alone. That was the face I hoped to remember him by.

"And Mary Read?" I wondered aloud to Maura as we walked beside each other. "Does that come from Mad Mary? That only seems to be a name John used to call you when you pissed him off."

After I had kissed John, I turned away to see Maura staring back at me with wild eyes and a slack jaw like she had just been slapped.

"He always pissed me off first," Maura muttered more to herself than me, and then she shrugged.

"Bonny Ann and Mad Mary. Anne Bonny and Mary Read. Who the fuck even are we, Maura?" I chuckled, low enough not to draw attention, but Maura's slight smile did not reach her eyes, and she looked away.

"Maura's not my Christian name, Ann."

I wanted to stop in my tracks, but being pulled along, I only tripped upon my clumsy, unused feet.

"What?" I asked dumbly.

"I was christened as a 'Mary.'"

"Oh," I said, glancing to the ground, even though Maura would still not look at me. "Then, where did 'Maura' come from?"

"My nan," she replied rapidly, a wistfulness clouding her far-off gaze. "I loved her dearly."

Her eyes cleared for a second and flickered towards me, now full of a subdued sorrow. "You're a lot like her. You both could tell good stories, because you both knew how to listen."

Color rose to my cheeks, and with the lack of any answer, Maura pushed on:

"I was named to honor her, my mother's mother, Maura, but my mam turned it into *Mary* instead. Told me years and years later that she did it to give me a better chance with 'English suitors.' Y'know, to have a name they recognized instead of a foreigner's. Even though they're just as foreign as me on these godforsaken islands . . . "

"So, you keep Maura as, like, a connection between you and your family, even though you're apart?"

"If I wanted to feel connected to them, Ann, I would not have left them," she finally faced me, furrowing her brows before forcefully relaxing her face. "No, I *chose* Maura because . . . " She looked away again. "I don't know, it's who I am, s'pose."

"I see," I muttered, awfully awkward once more. There was something left unsaid in her words, some traitorous thing that had always lived between the spaces of her words when she spoke of her past. Inhaling fully and lowering my voice further, I delicately broached: "Why did you leave them, Maura? You never told me."

Maura stiffened all of a sudden, but sighting my sincerity, she soon sighed in surrender. "I had a decent life, Ann. I don't have a sob story like everyone else. I just . . . wanted to. I had food, a home, only a little money, but enough to live on. My family didn't . . . *despise* me. My mam loved me enough, my nan rested peacefully in the ground, my siblings minded me, and my papa wasn't around to hurt or anythin'. It was a fine life, one many would kill fer, I'm sure. But it wasn't my life.

"I grew older, so I got more responsibilities. Mam worked, so I worked by feeding the kids, washing the clothes, trying to teach them what little knowledge I had gathered. When Mam was home, it was to tell me of all the young men, about marriage, a husband and seven children, just like her, just like everyone. And one night, as plain as any other, I was in bed with all my brothers and sisters, and I heard my mam come home and creak up the old stairs and slam her bedroom door, and I jolted up from the bed, my heart just poundin'. And it dawned on me: I didn't want this. I couldn't even think of what I did want, Ann, but I knew in my gut that it was *not* that. *Never* that. And within a quarter of an hour with what little coin I could find in the holey pockets of Papa's abandoned old coat, I was gone."

"It ate me up inside. I didn't regret it—and I still don't—and that was the problem. I thought about how miserable I must have made my mam, but I still didn't regret it. Sometimes I think about what might have happened if I had just stayed. If I had raised my siblings, gotten married, born children, raised them all over again, but then *I* would have been miserable.

"I hated myself, Ann," she shook her head, smiling incredulously, "fer being born selfish enough to be happy even when it made everyone else miserable. But then, I figured, if it's selfish to want to be happy, then everyone is selfish. Even my mam. Why does she get to be happy by forcing me to wed and birth and-and all that shite, and I don't? Why must I trade one misery fer another? Why is my happiness worth less?"

I wanted to stop walking; I wanted to hold

Maura's hand; I wanted to glide my fingers across her fragile waist and pull her close to me, so that my chest can be pressed against hers, our hearts aligned, and then she might finally hear how my own only beats to the sound of her laughter.

"Your happiness matters, Maura."

But I couldn't get what I wanted.

"Och, yea," she scoffed, "you're one to talk."

My breath caught; my teeth ground together; my eye twitched; my entire body protested against my ears.

"What is that supposed to mean."

"Och, Ann, you lie with a latchet," she taunted. "*You* can't even tell me when you've had a bad dream. What could *you* tell me about worth, about happiness?"

"I'm ... I'm ... "

I'm what? I wondered. *Was I not an innate sinner who deserved to be damned? Was I not that Anne Bonny, a criminal, a thief, a damned pirate?*

"It's different, with me."

"Yea?" She swiveled on her feet to look at me, stooping slightly to my lower height, mere inches from my face. She was flushed with anger. "How? What makes you *so* different?"

Or was I Ann Fulford, the babe born by a bitch, the girl with hair as red as the Devil's arse? A woman who betrayed her own sex, who never loved a man, who never bore the pains of Eve, who dabbled in alternative sin rather than weave herself into the predetermined loom of life?

"Because *I'm* different, Maura! I just *am different.*"

What did that girl's happiness matter? She was doomed to this death on the day of her birth.

"But I'm different, too, Ann. I'm different. Just. Like. *You.*"

All at once, my thoughts cleared, and I looked at her. I mean I *really* looked at her. I could record the pores on her face, the slight wrinkles lining her eyes, her mouth that thinned in rage, and her eyes ablaze in defiance of me.

"Tell me, Ann, and tell me honestly, if you can't damn well be truthful: *Do we deserve this?*"

My mouth dried. My tongue glued itself to my gums and would not budge, trapping my gross breath behind my rotting teeth, and I said nothing.

"Blood and 'ounds, Ann!" Maura broke and yelled to the ceiling, her eyes wettening and reddening. "Just feckin' talk to me! No more metaphors, no more stories, none of your break-teeth words. Tell me how you *feel*, goddammit! You just feckin' stew in your own suffering and you won't let anyone help, and you let some tallow-breeched, crab-lanthorned, harloting, flashy, flumping, windy, wambling, war-capering *buck fitch*, three skips of a louse, lay his lips on yours when you deserve the whole feckin' *world* and you don't even—"

Her words were cut short when, with a *whoosh* that cut through the still, moldy air, the butt of one of the soldier's muskets *thwacked*

Maura on her right temple. She stumbled back from its impact, and she might have toppled over if it weren't for the rope that tugged her wrists forward. Her ear began to bleed.

"Would you shut the fuck up?" he spat at her. "For a woman, you have tongue enough for two sets of teeth. *Christ Almighty!*"

He turned around and dragged us further down the corridor, but everything that ran in my brain was not *if* I should kill him but *how.* Oh, how I sickly longed to kick the back of his knee, make him keel over, and wrap the rope around his neck and pull, pull, pull, until his face inflated and his eyes bulged out of his sockets. I could see it all in a twisted clarity, but it wasn't twisted, not then; it was preordained, *divine.* And I would tell him to beg. Not to me, but to *her.* He'd have to beg her to call me off, that only her satisfaction could make me stop, only her word could make me heel—

But Maura was also the one to tug on our binds and pull me out of that fantasy. I looked at her frowning face, vainly ignoring the blood that trickled down from her neck to her collar.

Stop fighting, she meant as she shook her head softly. *It's not worth it.*

It was worth it to me, apparently. I didn't give a damn about what would happen. Any consequence that flitted through my mind was worth proving my devotion to Maura. If the Lord Christ was just a sliver as good as Maura was to me, then I could finally see why his apostles were set to die for Him.

I could never prove to myself what I deserved. I saw my own shadow and begot evil into it. But Maura? Maura didn't deserve this.

But how could I prove that to her? What was there left to do? There we were, walking side by side, step by step to the silent thrum of a funeral march, until we would be sentenced to the air's suspension, to hang and to sway, to ward off the worldly deserters and to keep the sheep by moonlight. Oh, what did it matter, what did it matter . . .

I suffered, and I *stewed* in my suffering, because to suffer was safe; it was easy and predictable, with means and an end, so one would never have to change. To hope, well, Hope was malleable. Hope took *real guts*.

And I? I was a coward.

With my head bowed in shame, I walked on, and I did not look at her.

❊ ❊ ❊

AS WE APPROACHED THE ENTRANCE TO OUR FATEFUL ENDS, the leading man in front of us spoke a few words to the guards that attentively stood on either side of the well-secured double-door. Nodding, the two guards opened the doors for us. A burst of light from the sunlit room blinded Maura and me; we had not been outside of our cell for a month.

When we entered the side of the courtroom, my eyes quickly adjusted to the brightness and absorbed the room around me. The walls were fairly tall, a stark contrast to the low-ceilings I had been inhabiting, and large paneled windows facing the rising sun created morning shadows across the intricate wooden panels and beams above us. There were many rows of benches behind the wooden railing on our left, reminiscent of church pews. They weren't packed with people, but the allure of a pirate trial drew in a considerable audience. To the right were the esquires, serving as commissioners in the court. Twelve of them sat uninterested before us, each with gray or blond wigs of tight curls that flopped like hoe cakes on their shoulders. However, splitting right down the middle of them was a thirteenth man in an extravagant wooden chair that was carved like a grotesque, gauche throne. I judged him to have the highest rank of them all, wearing a wig without a single fraying hair out of place. Due to his status, he was certainly the president of the court.

We were led to the 'bar,' a wooden railing placed in front of the commissioners' large curving desk, altogether creating the shape of a half-circle. Space was left between the desk and the bar for two men to sit at a cramped table adorned with a dark green cloth; each of them scribbled furiously at their parchment with a long quill. We were placed beside the railing awkwardly. Our tied hands were vulnerably held out before us like sacrifices. I braced myself for a commissioner to come down from one of their seats and slash our wrists until we dropped dead into our own puddles of blood in front of everyone. I believed no amount of cruelty could surprise me.

We were still in the garments we were captured in; we had not bathed since that day. Our wretched appearances lived up to the expectations of the townspeople gathered.

"Now," the man we followed in shiny black shoes turned to us, "you must hearken to your charge."

"Register of the court, William Norris," the man in the throne addressed our guide by name. "Please exhibit the Articles against the prisoners."

"With pleasure, your Excellency," Norris, the man who retrieved us, replied, bowing slightly before opening his book and reading aloud its contents.

He slowly rambled through the King's many titles and claims of sovereignty over his empire, colonies he has rule over—such as Jamaica—and others he has not—France—proclaiming it as the will of God; the English were so conceited that they deluded themselves in a sense of God-given superiority. I tuned out this desperate boot-licking.

My ears perked up, however, when he mentioned the proclamation made by George I's predecessor, William III. *An Act for the more Effectual Suppression of Piracy,* made for the "trying, hearing, determining, and adjudging," Norris explained, "of all Piracies, Robberies, and Felonies committed in or upon the high sea, or any haven, river, creak, or place, where the Admiral of Admirals, have Power, Authority, or Jurisdiction, before his Excellency, Sir Nicholas Lawes, Knight, Captain, General, and Governor in Chief of Our said Lord King George, in and over His Majesty's island of Jamaica, and territories thereon depending in America, Chancellor and Vice Admiral of the same, etcetera . . . "

I rolled my eyes at the drawn out and repetitive words of the Register Norris. He nodded his head slightly while speaking this overabundant praise to the man in the throne, undoubtedly being Sir Lawes, a well-groomed man with spectacles perched on his nose that was as crooked as he seemed to be, and he, in turn, bowed his head to the audience, as if he was doing them a great service by simply acknowledging their presence.

I had first waved off these people, but this pompous formality was equal parts fascinating and disgusting. It was a battle of power and superiority, from every snide comment to the construction of the front and the placement of troops; how could you not feel lesser when peering up at thirteen large men from the floor? We were the sinners who begged to seemingly merciful but secretly cruel saints. Stab wounds and gunshots were impersonal, but it was this vicious condescension that pierced the skin and sliced the heart, for it was perfectly and personally crafted for you, revealing the wretch you are in comparison to whoever deemed you unworthy.

I remembered why I had forsaken this life before.

Without missing a beat, Norris carried on:

" . . . And others, Commissioners appointed, in the said Commission, by William Norris, Esquire, Register of said court—" he placed a hand on his chest to refer to himself, *the twat—* "duly appointed and sworn, against Mary Read and Anne Bonny, alias *Bonn,* late of the Island Providence, Spinsters, for Piracies, Felonies, and Robberies, committed by them, on the High Sea, and within the jurisdiction of this court, that is to say . . . "

Spinsters, I scoffed privately. Neither Maura nor I were married, and being in our twenties, that made us old hags in the eyes of the law or any person in this court. And yet, it is with no doubt that some very men in this room were unmarried, yet they were forgiven, envied even. They were *bachelors*, and they had a good many years until entering their forties to even earn the epithet of *old.*

No, they wanted us to be the unlucky women who had nothing to live for, no husband to tend to, sitting alone in a house or on the street weaving thread on a spinning wheel with crusted, gnarled, veiny hands. But we refused. We deviated from their ideal, and now we were to be punished.

Norris cleared his throat with a breathy *"ahem"* and moved down his paper, reading:

" . . . That they, the said Mary Read and Ann Bonny, alias *Bonn—" where the hell did they get that 'Bonn',* I thought to myself— "and each of them, on the first day of September, in the Seventh Year of the Reign of our said Lord the King—" *get on with it!* — "that is now, upon the high sea, a certain Sloop, of an unknown name, being . . . "

The sloop's official name was the *William,* but that was the name the previous owner gave it before Dick "appropriated" it. He always called it *The Iron Fist,* an homage to Jackie, I presumed. He was incredibly reluctant to part with it once we encountered the *Mary,* and he fought mercilessly with Rackum to keep it, even raising a sword to duel one time. Jackie was the one to bring him down from his rage.

" . . . did feloniously and wickedly consult, and agree together, and to and with, John Rackam, George Fetherston, Richard Corner, John Davies, John Howell, Patrick Carty, Thomas Earl, and Noah Harwood, to rob, plunder, and take all such persons, as well subjects of our said Lord the King . . . "

I bowed my head at the sound of the names of my dead companions, hoping to hide my cheeks that quickly reddened with emotion. To hear their names spoken as if they were not once living souls that were expended, but instead animals being listed off, having been led to death by the lead that hung from their necks. *They dare call forth their ghosts,* I thought, *with such contempt for their souls.*

Norris, the Register, then spoke of the third of September, the date of our first plunder, when we had first set sail from Providence:

" . . . distant of about two leagues from Harbour-Island in America, and within the jurisdiction of this court, did piratically, feloniously, and in an hostile manner, attack, engage, and take, seven certain fishing-boats, then being, boats of certain persons, subjects of our said now Lord the King . . . "

It wasn't the grandest, most harrowing raid, as we were mostly in dire need of supplies to sustain our crew. While sailing, we had stumbled upon many fishermen about their usual haunts in the morning. There were a good number of boats, dotting the sea like a school of fish and their nets dragging along behind them like fins; some congregated together, some were out far into the waves, alone. Those were the ones we targeted.

" . . . and then and there, piratically, and feloniously, did steal, take, and carry away, the fish, the fishing-tackle, of the value of ten pounds, of current money of Jamaica, the goods and chattels of aforesaid fishermen, then and there upon the high sea aforesaid, in the aforesaid place . . . "

I had pitied some of these fishermen who were at the wrong place at the wrong time. They were simple folk like how most of us had once been. They would have been set farther back by our robberies than any wealthy merchant in a richer sloop, but we were desperate men who had been starving for three days, and desperate men turned vicious in the face of need. Besides, Rackum was not one to discriminate between his victims, no matter their circumstance. We followed his lead.

It was two days after this raid when Governor Rogers, that same man that pardoned Rackum for his crimes, had issued a proclamation calling for the arrest of 'John Rackum' and crew, listing many of us by name, including myself.

Odd, I thought. *They had called me Ann Fulford in that paper.*

We sailed idly around the Caribbean after that, picking on the stray ship that wandered too far from its harbor. It was wrong, we all knew that, but our morals were a price we were willing to pay for the freedom from a pitiful life. Then, Norris brought up the excursion we partook in almost a month later, on the first of October, when we neared the island of Hispaniola:

" . . . did piratically, and feloniously, set upon, shoot at, and take, two certain merchant sloops, then being sloops of certain persons, subjects of our said Lord the King and then and there," he exclaimed again, waving his free hand in the air in a flourishing motion as if he was reaching an ecclesiastical climax in a certain sermon, "piratically! and feloniously! did make an assault, in and upon, one James Dobbin, and certain other mariners . . . "

Dobbins, I thought of his name, or at least I thought of the name he gave us. He was a simple sailor on board the day we boarded his ship, one of the many we rounded up as we pillaged and plundered. He was no different than the rest of them, cowering with the rest of the shiphands. However, he showed enough courage, or he at least showed the right amount of rashness that came to a man when he realized he had nothing to lose, and he volunteered to be a part of our crew, separating himself from his mates and approaching us himself. Rackum was not in the market for extra hands, but he was impressed by the man's gumption and decided to take him on board. We were lucky to have him. At least, I counted myself lucky. He became one of my dearest friends in the end.

" . . . piratically, and feloniously," Norris repeated again for emphasis, "did steal, take, and carry away, the said two merchant sloops, and the apparel and tackle of the same sloops, of the value of one thousand pounds of current money of Jamaica . . . "

While we had come away with the most impressive sum we would ever get, the sloops themselves, each expertly crafted with two masts, were built for duration and cargo, not for the speed which we deeply desired in a ship on the sea. I had wanted to just let the ships go with their masters, as we had taken more than enough for ourselves, but Rackum quickly grew paranoid. He was afraid that they could easily give chase to us or warn the Navy, and he hastily gave the orders to have both ships sunk by our cannons and to send the crews ashore on their little dinghies. We had left them there, bobbing up and down on the waves, and they watched us sailing away. I remembered Dobbins standing beside me on the prow and we watched his past mates disappear into the horizon; he was the first of us to turn away.

Then, Norris spoke of our next raid, the one large enough to last two days, starting on the nineteenth day of October at Porte-Maria Bay, on the other side of Jamaica:

" . . . did piratically, feloniously, and in a hostile manner, shoot at, set upon, and take, a certain schooner, of an unknown name, whereof one Thomas Spenlow was Master . . . "

Thomas Spenlow was a Brandy-faced arse, as full as a goat stewing in a casque of wine. He was already half-seas over by the time we got to his schooner, a pathetic thing with a single failing mast and a sparse crew. Needless to say, it was no laborious task to overcome his ship.

" . . . and then and there piratically and feloniously, did steal, take, and carry away the said schooner, the apparel and tackle of the same schooner, of the value of twenty pounds of current money in Jamaica . . . "

We hauled Spenlow's schooner behind us, and as there was little to take from his person, we kept Spenlow hostage, yet we doubted anyone who tripped over himself and knocked himself unconscious when first boarding our ship would garner any sort of ransom.

We saw differently on the twentieth day of October when we had sailed by Jamaica:

" . . . did piratically, feloniously, and in a hostile manner," the Register particularly enunciated for the umpteenth time, "set upon, board, and enter, a certain merchant sloop called the *Mary*, then being a sloop of certain persons, whereof Thomas Dillon, mariner, was master . . . "

Thomas Spenlow's fellow, Thomas Dillon, was harbored near where we had our eyes set in Dry Harbor Bay. It was madness to issue another attack only a day after our previous one, but Rackum was never one to follow rationality. He entered one of his moods where his mind told him that the ship was coming to get Spenlow, that they knew what we were and knew what "our sins" entailed. He ordered fire upon the vessel.

He's off the hooks, I thought when he stood at the prow with a murderous fire flaring in his eyes. But as I stood in my own trial and recalled what transpired before, I wondered how much of his mind was shaped by his original surrender to Governor Rogers for his piracy. He had put an even larger target on his back by returning to the seas, and whether or not his skittishness was product of his fear of being trapped and tied down once more, I could not be sure.

Seagull tried to challenge him, but John whispered something into his ear, whether some threat, some bargain, or some Godforsaken reason, but Seagull complied and backed up Rackum. We had no authority to question either of them, so we launched an attack upon the sloop.

" . . . and then and there!" said he, a preacher damning the wicked, "piratically, and feloniously, did steal, take, and carry away, the said sloop *Mary*, and the apparel and tackle of the same sloop, of the value of three hundred pounds, in current money of Jamaica . . . "

Dick's ship had been properly scraped up in the skirmish, with one of our masts being blown to bits and holes puncturing the side of our ship, and we had to lay it to rest in the waves. We took the *Mary*, a decent sloop, with two masts even sturdier than our own, although we lost many of the guns we had equipped on *The Iron Fist*. We only realized this issue once we had been properly attacked by the English.

Norris had finished reading through the articles while my mind had been occupied with the memories of the past, the ones I reminisced and the ones I regretted. But it was of no matter then. I had made my decision many months ago, and now, I was going to pay for it. No mere recollection could change the course my life had taken. I had accepted that, but I had not yet accepted dying for it. And as I looked over to where Maura stood beside me, despite her high talk of honor and death, I don't think she had accepted it either.

"What have you to say? Whether you are guilty of the piracies, robberies, and felonies, or any of them, in the same Articles mentioned, which have been then read unto you? Or not guilty?"

Maura's eyes bulged out of her skull, like a bug someone had wrapped thick fingers around and squeezed. It was a peculiar look on her face, one that conveyed all the emotions she would never admit to.

Her lips, already thin, were pressed into a straight line, holding back all the words she wanted to say. Yet, when she opened her mouth, her breath hitched; her throat had dried up as she fought within herself, her desire for glory battling with her instinct for survival.

I had never seen her so vulnerable, so weak, bloodied and beaten and marred by their hands, and it hurt my heart to see her crumble at the cruelty of the court. *They* had no right to see her like this, to break her like this. I could not bear it any longer, so I turned to the Register.

"Not guilty," I answered for her.

"And you, Mary Read? Do you plead the same?"

Norris sighed, clearly disappointed by our answer, before turning to Maura and asking her directly. I looked at her again, and I noted the emotion that swirled in her eyes. I could not quite place what they were trying to tell me, whether it be fear or betrayal or relief.

Maura gulped dryly and told the Register:

"Not Guilty."

"Well then," Norris said while handing the Articles to the page boy who then scurried out of the room. "I call and produce the witnesses to prove the said Articles and charge against the prisoners, to be examined by His Excellency, the President, and the Court, in the presence and hearing of the prisoners. I first call forth Thomas Spenlow to depose at the stand."

Spenlow looked just as I remember him, a gundiguts with a full beard and ill-fitting clothes that stretched over his belly. Although, he was considerably more sober, even if by force. He still lumbered towards the steps of the stand with a dazed, hung-over countenance. He was elevated on the wooden stand, hastily made without a varnish or proper securing. It creaked as he shifted his weight before settling.

After he was sworn in, Norris began to question:

"Tell us, Master Spenlow, what transpired when you were captured."

"Y'know, I told e'ryone last time," he said gruffly, rubbing his eyes.

"Yes, but would you be so kind, sir, as to tell us again?"

"Well," Spenlow blinked, clearly trying to remember what had happened when he had been mauled by booze that evening, "they, uh, fired a gun at me and boarded my ship, and I was ta'en by, uh, Rackam, and I was kep' on his sloop for two days when they attack ed Dillon."

"And the females? The prisoners at the bar?"

"Oh, uh," he squinted at Maura and me. "They womenfolk was there, they, uh, they was there on the sloop."

"Is that all, Master Spenlow?"

"Look, I tol' ya e'rything those last two trials!" He barked impatiently. "What more can a feller spew?"

"That will be all, Master Spenlow. You are dismissed."

Thomas Dillon was called upon next, once sworn, he gripped the sides of the stand and leaned forward, as if preparing the audience for a captivating tale.

"I was lying at Anchor in Dry Harbor with the sloop Mary and Sarah—oh, what beaut's they were!"

I had not interacted with Dillon before, but he was clearly a man who loved the sound of his own voice.

" . . . and a strange sloop came into the said harbor—but a strange ship comes every now and again so I didn't think much of it, until it fired a gun at me sloop! And then I remembered, Spenlow didn't pull in last night, and I told meself, *Hark, Thomas, there be some skullduggery afoot!* And that's when I realized, *Good Lord! Pirates!*" He gasped before this last comment, throwing his hands in the air in a theatrical performance, but his audience did not startle nor cheer.

"We had to go ashore, me and my men, to defend ourselves and our ship. So, after several shots had been fired at us, I hailed 'em, and one guy, they called him like . . . enh, I don't remember. He was that feller with that kind of hang-gallows look, with the sunken cheeks and the patchy brown beard . . . " Dillon stroked his own stubbled face where a beard would have been.

"Are you referring to George Fetherstone?" Norris interjected.

"Oh, er . . . Yes! It was him, I believe. So Fetherstone answered me, and he said that we need not be afraid, and that him and his crew, they desired me to come on board their ship. Who was I to refuse? Not when they had a cannon to me head." He laughed, amused with himself, even when no one laughed with him. "So, I went on board and saw that the ship was commanded by John Rackam! It was bizarre to be among pirates, but all kind of dull to be honest. Only one of them had those peg legs, and none of them had barnacles for warts. Well, afterwards, he and his crew took me sloop and her lading, and carried her off with them to sea . . . "

The morning after that successful plunder was supposed to be one of idle and self-congratulatory leisure as we would plan our next route, but when we awoke, we found our supplies to be ravaged in turn. Tobacco, fishing tackle, a dinghy and a pair of oars were all missing, along with the disappearance of one, Andrew Gibbons.

Andrew had been Maura's lover, and Rackum was to question Maura about what she knew of Andrew's whereabouts and motives, but one look at her slack face as she came out of her slumber to search for her mate had told the rest of us all we needed to know. She fled below deck for the remainder of the day, and threatened Rackum with a pistol when he tried to get her to work. We all gave her a wide berth that day as she hid herself. The next day when she emerged, she went back to swabbing the deck and climbing the masts, as though nothing had happened. It was when one tried to talk with her that the venom would seep from her voice. Andrew may have left us, but he abandoned her.

"Oh, yes, and the two women prisoners," Dillon stumbled out of his storytelling to remember why he was actually there. "They were on board Rackam's sloop, I think I remember that . . . Anne, Bonny Anne, had a gun in her hand. Yes," he said, looking squarely at me and nodding as if he was regarding a poorly painted picture, "it was her. Can't mistake that ghastly red hair, can you? Oh, but both women were very profligate, cursing and swearing much," he swished his hand in the air before his eyes lit up and he grinned devilishly, saying " . . . and ready to do any Thing on board."

Dillon laughed to himself at his lewd joke, and the crude stand on which he stood on shook with the force of his rumbling chuckle. Other men in the audience laughed too, even one of the Commissioners, yet they subdued it enough in the courtroom setting where the laughter was simply hollow, mirthless and mocking. Maura's lip twitched at the remark, and I tried to pull back the heat that crawled over my complexion.

Dillon was dismissed, as John Besneck and Peter Cornelian were called forth together, but being Frenchmen, they were translated by Simon Clarke, a neatly pert man in spectacles who stood at the base of the stand. All were sworn in.

As the Frenchmen talked animatedly to themselves, Clarke kept track and repeated their words in English once they steadied their speech:

"As we were out hunting," Clarke began as

the French chattered on, "for the Hog . . . off the shore of the island of Hispaniola in America, the crew of Rackam stole us . . . and brought us onto their ship as prisoners."

I finally remembered why those toads looked so familiar. They did, after all, look very different in the broad daylight beyond the brig without vomit staining their uniforms.

"During this time, the two females of the bar . . . were on board Rackam's sloop while Rackam took control of Spenlow's schooner and Dillon's sloop. When they saw any vessel . . . the women gave chase or attacked, and they wore men's clothes. The red hair girl handed gun powder to the men."

I did a lot more than that, and you know it, I thought, looking squarely at the first one's right shoulder that slumped slightly ever since I stabbed it. It was one thing to be beaten by a woman and another to admit it to a crowd of men.

"They did not seem to be kept or detained by force . . . but of their own free will and consent. They were very active on board, and . . . " Clarke trailed away as the French began to hurriedly talk back and forth between themselves. Clarke looked at them in shock as they tittered away like birds about *"le petit Jésus."* When there came a pause, Clarke bashfully informed the commissioners:

"They are . . . reasserting Master Dillon's comment, they too say they were very *active* on board and were willing to do any . . . Thing."

I lowered my head and bit back my embarrassment as roars of laughter rang all around me. I could not bear to see their leering, judging, ogling gazes, even though I felt them all on me in waves of sticky heat. *We're either prudes or we're whores*, I thought to myself. *Both will be scorned. Both will be coveted. Such is the fate of being a woman in this manly world.*

Then, a woman was called up onto the stand. *Odd*, I thought, for what my old mates told me of their trial, there were only male witnesses. They must have wanted to leave the women for each other.

She was a nervous thing, hands wringing above her most modestly clad chest. She had on a plain white bonnet that gave the impression of youth until one looked under its brim and witnessed her sunken eyes and graying face. It was those intense eyes that made me remember who she was. Her name was said to be Dorothy Thomas.

"I was at sea with some stock and provisions," she began with a timid, trembling voice, "at the North side of Jamaica. I was doing a bit of fishing for my husband, John. He came down with a fever, but nothing too great. He was spared and returned to me, thank the Lord, but during that time, I had to take on his duties, even if it wasn't the proper thing for a respectable lady to do. I was going through the motions, spreading out the fishing net and waiting diligently, until I was taken by a sloop commanded by that . . . sinful man, God Have Mercy on his Soul. I did not know his name, but I afterwards heard from the good folk of Harbor Island that it was John Rackam. His men and those . . . women attacked me while he took most of the things that were in my canoe."

It came back to me, the shrieking woman who shook uncontrollably during our plunder of the large gathering of fishermen. (It wasn't terribly uncommon to find a woman among fishermen, especially when the empty bellies of children were waiting back home.) She swiftly went into a feverish hysteria at the sight of us pirates, but she had settled into an even more calm, disturbing loathing when she spotted me and Maura.

"Lord, yes!" She finally looked at us with crazed eyes and grimacing teeth. "Those two women were on board, the she-devils. They wore men's jackets and long trousers and handkerchiefs tied around their heads. They wanted to be men!" She laughed at this apparent absurdity, but the laugh echoed across the walls and high ceilings like the strained cry of a seagull flying with a broken wing. "Each of them had a cutlass and pistol in their rough and calloused hands, men's hands, and oh, my! They were out to get me, I tell you all!" Her head darted around the room, accusing all who did not believe her.

"They cursed and swore at the men to murder me! That they should kill me to prevent me from coming against them!"

I wanted to laugh at this woman or fight

her for claiming something so far from the truth, something only existing in her imagination. But, there was only pity to be held for a woman like her, who so succumbed to the cruelty of being a servant to men that she was utterly shattered by the idea that someone could break through the chains she considered immovable. She had bent her back over other men for so long that when she saw a woman standing up on her own, her resolve cracked, and she could only crumble to the ground.

"Because I, a woman, saw them for what they truly were. They defied their God-given nature and rebelled against Him and His gifts, but I saw through it. I could tell they were women by the largeness of their breasts. They couldn't escape it, I tell you. *They couldn't escape it!*"

She burst into sobs on the stand, but they were dry gasps of air, full of tears that would never come.

"That will be all, Mistress Thomas," Norris said to her, more confused than concerned, and he had a page take her by the hand and lead her down the stand. Male voices in the audience began to murmur among themselves, sharing sentiments of confusion, condescension, and annoyance. Even I, her accused, had more compassion for her than these men did.

The President, Sir Lawes, called for order to be restored in the court, slamming a gavel down on a block on his desk. The room was quieted, and the president had the floor to query.

"Prisoners of the bar," he spoke in a deep, droll voice, uninterestedly going through the customary actions, "do you, either or both, have any defense to make, any witnesses to be sworn on your behalf? Or, would you have any of the witnesses, who had already been sworn, cross-examined? If you would, propose and declare to the court what questions you both, or either of you would have asked. If you have any, the Court, or myself, will interrogate them."

He looked at me from behind his crooked nose, staring down at us as if we were cockroaches he longed to stomp beneath his boot. I searched around the room for a face I recognized or one that I could consider friendly, but there came none. Stuck amidst the gaze of a hundred, every eye lingered on me, and every person waited with bated breath for our downfall. It was intimidating, being forced to defend myself among a sea of enemies. No one would ever listen to me; my words would be dismissed, and my tears would pool absently on the ground with no one to care. Thus, I sheepishly turned away.

And there was Maura, who did care, who cared, perhaps, too much. Looking at me with an expression both pleading and regretful, I took a deep breath and addressed the court:

"We have no witnesses, nor any questions to ask," I choked out, and I cursed the frailty in my voice, but I ceased when I realized it didn't matter. It never did. Weakness or strength meant nothing to these men. Everything rode on how you were made. That determined who you were, what life you were supposed to live, and how you were destined to die.

"As that is the case," Sir Lawes spoke, "may the guards take the prisoners from the bar and put them into safe custody. All the standers withdraw from the court, save for the Register . . . "

The two guards that had been a few footsteps behind us each grabbed me and Maura by the arms and shoved us to the door from whence we came. I could hear the shuffling of men getting up from their seats, having been excused to debate the matter of our lives, and the echoes of conversation, but soon, we were back in the hallway, and the sound of the door closing behind us, swiftly shutting away the tense hustle we had been in the midst of, reverberated off the cold walls. Soon enough, that noise was hushed too, and we were escorted to our cell in the silent candlelight.

❋ ❋ ❋

TEARS GATHERED LIKE DEW DROPS ON MAURA'S LASHES the moment we were deposited to a holding cell. Once our ropes were removed, Maura slumped to the floor, sinking to her knees in a fluid motion and pressing her palms to her eyes. I crouched down in front of her.

"Ann," she said to me as I lowered her wrists from her face. When Maura's eyes opened and flashed at me, I could see how they had turned a soft, puckered crimson from her crying. Some last composure broke within Maura when she looked at me, and when her head collapsed upon my shoulder, she started to sob.

"I couldn't do it, Ann. I don't want to die."

"No one really does," I muttered uselessly as I rubbed my cheek against the curling hairs on her head. She pressed her closed eyes against my neck, and I couldn't tell if the wet warmth trickling down my collarbone was because of the tears, the sweat, or the blood from her temple.

"Yea, you say that, everyone feckin' says that. Ann, there have been times when I've looked forward to death, either having it close or far off. Whether miserable or content, I always believed that when finally faced with my end, I would have done everything in my power to have the life I wanted, and that would be enough." Her voice went down to a whisper. "It's not enough, Ann. There is so much more I haven't done, things I've never had that will be lost to me forever. So much right here, Ann . . . "

Her words faded away on her tongue until there was nothing left between her ragged, staggered breaths and my bare skin. In our clutched hands, Maura began stroking my knuckles with a delicate thumb before she sighed.

"I suppose you wouldn't understand," she said with a closed finality, withdrawing from my hands and from her place on my shoulder.

"I do," I said just as quickly, grabbing Maura's retreating hands tightly. She was frigid at the fingertips. "I-I do understand, Maura."

We exchanged something in silent glances, but I was unsure of what was being said. She looked up at me with glossy eyes, the whites fading and veiny with the salty residue, but I didn't know what she wanted. Every voice was screaming within me to comfort her, to hold her and hide her away from this world that made devils out of us. Suddenly, when a single tear fell across her cheek, those voices became one, and it told me what I was going to do.

I closed the gap between us and grazed my lips gently across her temple, the place where she was hit and where the awful blood was drying, kissing her with the delicacy and care I knew had never been offered to her. I offered myself now.

Then pressing our foreheads together, I closed my eyes and committed to memory that feeling of being in someone's space, of minds passing through bone and skin and melding into something immortal. It was a greeting and a goodbye all in one, and it would be the sole thing I would carry with me as I walk into my grave.

I chanced it all and opened my eyes briefly

to study Maura's reaction, and I found her gazing back at me in turn. There was evident sorrow, but there was a sort of undercurrent wonder present too, like the sure and impossible sound of a river running in a ravine beneath my feet.

She smiled at me. No teeth; only a small tug at the lips and the pinching of eyes.

We're going to die soon, I thought, smiling too, *and I don't want to die without having this.*

* * *

OUR NECKS WERE BARED TO OUR PROSPECTIVE EXECUTIONERS while we stood at the bar, looking up at the men who passed our lives around like it was an exquisite tobacco to be tried. We were silently scrutinized by those thirteen men until the president announced from where he sat:

"The Commissioners and I have taken the evidence which have been given against the prisoners into consideration, and having maturely and deliberately considered thereof and of the circumstances of the prisoners' case, we have unanimously agreed that Mary Read and Ann

Bonny, alias *Bonn,* are both of them *guilty* of the Piracies, Robberies, and Felonies charged against them in the Third and Fourth Articles, of the Articles aforesaid."

The president looked at us truly for the first time during the trial. My shoulders slacked under the weight of his verdict:

"I now ask whether you, or either of you, have anything to say or offer why Sentence of Death should not pass among them for your said offenses?"

Maura and I stayed silent. *Nothing can be done,* the thought echoed in my mind. *It's over.* I had to submit to my fate once again, and I winced at the expected blow of the words to come:

"*YOU,*" Sir Lawes bellowed as he stood from his chair, "Mary Read *and* Ann Bonny, *alias* Bonn . . . "

"Stop," Maura whispered beside me.

" *. . . are to go from hence to the Place from whence you came, and from thence to the Place of Execution . . .* "

"Please stop," she uttered a little louder. The guards took notice.

" *. . . where you shall be severally hang'd by the neck, 'till you are severally dead.*"

"Wait," she said then, attracting the attention of the first row of observers.

"And GOD of His infinite Mercy be merciful to both of your souls."

"*I plead the belly!*" Maura shouted at last,

garnering looks from the Commissioners and spectators alike. Even I looked at her just as frantically, mouth agape.

Maura collapsed to the court floor, wilting, sinking like a trampled flower onto the ground. Kneeling, the only thing left to prop her up was the wooden bar fixed beneath her elbows. Her head lowered to her clasped hands, chafing red by the poor rope, and she rested her forehead against her entwined fingers, forced together prayerfully. I was confused, startled, and so very terrified, but nevertheless, I followed suit, kneeling beside her, so that she may not feel alone in front of the accursed crowd.

And there were we: two convicts, two criminals; two deadmen, two devils; two spinsters, two whispers; two friends, two fiends; whatever the world saw us to be. There, we made the bar into our communion rail, and the curved desk into the altar where we were sacrificing our blood and body. The whole court room was a chancel, but I didn't pray, to them or to God or to anyone, and I don't think Maura did either. She was, however, at her own confession:

"I am quick with Child," was all she said before her head rose to stare at me. "We both are."

CHAPTER 5:

The Girl I Left Behind Me

"WHAT THE FUCK, MAURA?" I ASKED HER as soon as we were brought to our cell and left to our own devices. Because of Maura's confession, the execution of our sentence had been respited until a 'further inspection' could be made. "Why the hell did you do that?"

"To save our skins, Ann," she spat back at me as I paced back and forth. "They've delayed our hanging. That's all that matters."

"All that matters?" I stopped to look at her incredulously. "Nothing bloody matters! Did you even stop to think about what would happen when the jury of matrons comes and finds out that there is no baby? They'll still kill us once they find out we've lied—"

"Who says I've lied?" Maura finally snapped,

stepping forward into my still space. "I haven't bled since September, Ann."

Everything came crashing down at once before it all rose up again and forced its way out of my mouth. I threw up onto the floor.

"Blood and 'ounds, Ann!" Maura yelped as she jumped back. "Could y'give a little warning before you spew everywhere?"

I stayed hunched over, facing the floor for many seconds, breathing rapidly, but no matter what I did, it felt like no air ever reached my lungs. The acidic taste of last night's meal that dissolved into mulch lingered on the roof of my mouth, and I watched as some strings of clear bile dripped down from my nose. I was too stunned to react, too afraid to speak.

"Andrew." My eyes unfocused as I pulled together the missing pieces. "He . . . before he left . . . " I absentmindedly wiped my mouth.

"Yes, Ann," Maura said as she tiptoed around my puke to pull me up by the shoulders and face her. "Yes, it was Andrew."

"Why didn't you tell me?"

"I didn't know! Thought the bleeding was a blip, y'know? But then, I felt a . . . squirming. Thought it was a worm, at first." She joked, but it fell flat on my ears, and her face dropped along with her chuckle.

"And even then, you still didn't tell me?"

"I don't know, Ann! I was frightened."

"Frightened? Of me?"

"No! . . . Yes. I don't know. But I had good reason to be frightened if the news would make you flay the fox."

"Because," I gritted through my teeth, "now you're carrying *Andrew's* babe."

"Bollox, Ann," she muttered with a red face. She then laughed in my face with a maniacal energy, and her shoulders shuddered with sparks crackling underneath her skin. "Is that what you're hung up on? That's rich coming from you."

"What the hell is that supposed to mean?"

"Oh please, you say that as if I *betrayed you* somehow, while you went ahead and kissed John-*feckin'*-Rackum—"

"He was about to die, Maura! Do I send a man to be capered without one thing to be happy about? Should I deny a dead man his last request?"

"*Yes!*" Maura nearly screamed in my face, burning crimson and brimming with tears, but she took a step backwards. "You—I . . . och, feck it, Ann." She wiped her face with her palm.

"You know it meant nothing, Maura," I sighed, but some bitter snake slithered through my stomach; its forked tongue licked at venomous words that whispered *danger, danger, back away and run.* It made me hiss and cross my arms defensively: "And why would you care?"

She laughed pitifully at this question and refixed her watery gaze at the cracking ceiling. "You know exactly why, Ann. Don't deny it. You know how I feel about you."

I did. I did know, no matter how much I told myself I didn't. It was a large force pushing on me, pressing down on the walls I've fortified myself in. I felt it with every smile that alighted her face when she found me, the rare warmth when she held me in her arms, the spark that ignited her eyes when she gazed upon me. It was that same spark that shone in her eyes now, but it was dim with the shade of rejection.

My defense was breaking; the walls I've surrounded myself were cracking, and vines were creeping through the mortar, pulling apart the stones one by one until they began to crumble. Feelings blossomed into flowers, the ones I tried so hard to starve and I held onto the last blade to cut them down before they could surround me with the aroma of hope: "Andrew's *claimed* you, Maura."

"Claimed? *Claimed?* Is that what you feckin' think?" I leaned back as she took a couple short steps to crowd my face. "That is disgusting—I refuse to let any of myself be *claimed* by that fecker who-who used me for a *good time*, a-and then just snuck out in the dead of night. No, that son-of-a-bitch has no claim over me. He forfeited any right the moment he abandoned me. Is that what you honestly thought?"

"I thought . . . I thought you . . . " *I thought you could be mine,* my heart murmured, but I quickly killed those words before they reached my tongue. *No, I can't let you. I won't.*

"I didn't want to get pregnant with that

lobcock's seed. What . . . " she waved her hands around, as if trying to grasp at her words in the air, and paced around the cell. "Did you think I was going to get pregnant and then gall-a-vant off with him into the sunset, settle down in a house in the grass where I milk the cows like a good little wife? Don't be ridiculous. I will not be made into a wife, Ann, and I sure as hell would not be made into his."

"I don't know what I thought," I weakly muttered, but even I could not hear my own words over the deafening beating of my heart.

"Heed me now: this baby is not his; *I* am not his," Maura paused and stood in the corner, inhaling deeply to settle her nerves. "This was not something I planned, Ann. I didn't want this baby."

She panted, exhausted of fury, and turned away from me to collect herself. Once calmed, she approached me with a serious determination and diverted the topic:

"Look, Ann, I didn't want this baby, but it has come as a blessin'. It will spare us from the gallows—"

"Us? *Us?* What are you talking about?" I shouted. "You, sure, but me? What about me, Maura? We can't fake a pregnancy with me. The matrons will see through it."

"They won't touch you. I'll be sure of it."

Despite her unwavering voice, her confident countenance broke when she met my eyes. Her shoulders slouched the moment she saw something in my eyes.

"Why don't you trust me?" She asked at last.

"I-I do trust you!"

"Then why do you always *pull away from me!*"

My eyes widened with shock as her voice cracked, and a single tear dripped down her face. I instinctively raised a hand to wipe it away, but I withdrew when my mind caught up with me.

"I'm . . . I'm sorry, Maura" I gently said. "I shouldn't have . . . I don't mean to pull away from you."

"Yes, you do," Maura immediately spat back.

"Yea," I hung my head cowardly, "I suppose I do."

Every day felt dark and bleak. Every day reminded me of what awaited beyond the veil, of all I could never have in life and all I could be denied in death. It was like the chime of a clock vibrated through my bones with every stroke of the passing day, and with every toll I felt myself fading, becoming more and more of a pointless specter that wandered aimlessly and alone inside my own dilapidated cage.

Maura was the only thing left in color. When the rest of the world fell to shadow, she was there to shine. The thought of that light extinguishing was enough to make me collapse then and there into Maura's open arms.

"I'm so fucking afraid, Maura." My bottom lip quivered as I stammered out the thoughts that raced through my head. "I don't want to die. I don't want *you* to die. I don't want to lose you. I can't handle it. I am being torn apart every day with suspense. I *can't* love you, Maura. I won't let myself, I won't. I can't bear loving you and losing you. I just *can't.* My heart will stop if I watch you die . . . "

My vision clouded with tears, and I sank to the ground away from Maura, bringing my knees to my chest. I wanted to hide away. I felt naked, but this nakedness ran deeper than exposing my skin. I had taken a knife to my chest, sawed a hole into my ribs' cage, and extracted my bleeding heart. Then splitting my heart in two like an apple, I showed Maura the blackened pit inside, the rooting seeds of my love for her and the guilty maggots that ate away at its flesh.

"Don't . . . make me . . . suffer any longer," I gasped between sobs.

"You don't have to suffer," Maura told me as she wrapped her arms around me and held my head against her breastbone.

"But I do . . . already."

"Because you won't allow yourself to feel anything else."

"What else is there? We're going to die. They'll hang us either way, delay or not."

"So they will," she said resolutely, gripping my shoulders as I flailed like a fish on a dock, "but they can't yet, and that'll buy us some time."

"To do what?"

Maura took my face in her hands. "To be,

Ann. To be together. We may die at the end, but knowing I've had some precious months to be by your side will make me believe it's all worth it, everything, and I will leave this Earth smilin'." She grinned without showing her teeth, but to me, she beamed like she had swallowed the sun. "The only thing we take with us when we die, Ann, is our memory. We may not remember once we're buried and in the bellies of worms, but we will die as the people that have been shaped by them. I can accept death knowing that I'll die as the Maura who loved you as you deserved."

My jaw trembled at the intense honesty Maura brought with her words, but I was still doubtful. I asked her the one thing that had been rattling around in my mind.

"Did you ever love *him*?"

This question took her by surprise, and cocking her head to the side, she stopped to consider her answer.

"No," she started slowly, "but I thought that with some time, I could. Time goes slow when you're walking this path alone . . . but I learned he was not the one I wanted by my side."

She gazed straight into my eye, and never before that moment had I felt so *seen*. Not even when I was judged, not even when I was admired. This was deeper; I had opened myself to her, heart exposed and vulnerable, but she found my soul and saw its shadows cutting through the light, or perhaps the rays that pierced through the dark.

I was neither good nor bad, that was true, and Maura saw that, and she decided that she would love all of me anyway.

"Will you have me, Ann? Will you let me love you? Will you let me be by your side from now until we walk the gallows together?"

Despite the fact I had spilled blood before, despite the fact that I had killed and stole and fought, *despite* the fact I stood behind bars in a sticky cell of mildew, I blushed like I was a girl of thirteen who had ribbons the color of pink roses in her hair. I smiled shyly, as if I had never smiled before.

I knew I had to stop running, to prop open my chest, and to let the vines take root and make a home.

"Yes," I said simply. That was all that needed to be said.

When we kissed, it was like the ceiling burst open, and I could see the stars again.

❊ ❊ ❊

I STOOD AT THE BOW OF A SHIP WEARING A NOOSE AS A NECKLACE. *My hands were tied, my feet were tied, and I was at the bow of the ship. I did not know who's ship it was. We were being sucked into a whirlpool. Charybdis, some seamen called it. It spun and sucked with a black sludge, and there were circling rows of teeth at the bottom of the vortex. Its breath stank. Maura was tied next to me. There was a rope connecting our bound wrists. The ship was jostled by the swirling sea, and Maura was knocked over into the abyss. I screamed, and I was pulled in with her. We fell into the gaping maw of Charybdis, yet no tooth scratched us. We eventually fell into the pool of squid ink at its center, and the ropes dissolved. I lost Maura as she sunk deeper into the ink. I dove down to find her until I felt something in the darkness. I pulled it up to the surface, and there was only a baby. The baby had flaming red hair, and boils erupted on its skin until it became a maroon-skinned devil. I tried to drown it, but the ink evaporated into clouds of smoke that the devil blew away, suspending us both in the thick darkness. It continued to grow and grow to the size of a mountain. It picked me up by the collar with its clawed hands. It squeezed its fingers around my neck until my eyes burst with blood. I turned to ash in its hands and floated away in a puff, forgotten . . .*

I awoke next to Maura, tense and stiff in her arms. My lungs shook with shallow breaths. *I'm safe,* I tried to tell myself as I sunk back into her dreaming embrace, but something else echoed back:

For now.

About a week had passed since our trial. We spent the time in companionable contentment as we reminisced on the sea, told stories of our past, and stole kisses when we could. We had nothing to do but laze around, no one to be, no one to answer to, so we decided to enjoy that small comfort while we could, but there was still a worry that gnawed on my cold bones, no matter how warm my heart was.

Suddenly, the door was rattled open, and two new guards led six women into the prison. The movement I made while entangling myself from Maura's arms woke her, and we both sat up.

This was *the jury of matrons*, selected by the Commissioners among the few women who observed our trial. They appeared to be working-class with their aprons fastened around their waists and cotton bonnets secured to their heads, and none of them had the money to afford patterned cloth for their dresses.

The grated door was unlocked, and the women filed into the cell. The guards locked it again and stayed in the room, but in an attempt to be modest, they turned their backs to us.

"Goodmorrow, m'dears," a kindly woman said as her thin wrinkled skin slid along her face. She bent down and began inspecting Maura first, turning her head this way and that.

"Ye poor thing," she tutted, "looking like Death's Head on a Mop-Stick."

"Oh, hush, Margaret," another one said behind her. She was a sharp-nosed lady, at least ten years younger than the other woman, Margaret, but she still had deep lines drawn from either side of her nose to the corners of her mouth. She dropped down to feel Maura's forehead. "We're not here to speak condolences."

"Yes," a well-groomed woman in a brown dress commented as she pressed herself to the exit, "lest you forget what these women are."

"Aye, but it's nae crime to be polite," the woman called Margaret said, wrapping a finger around Maura's wrist, feeling for a pulse.

"Were ye really a pirate, miss?"

This voice came from a young lass, no more than sixteen, I'd guess. She still had that naive twinkle to her warm brown eyes as she kneeled beside me.

"Yes," I answered in a hush, as if I was sharing a secret, "we were on the high seas together, where we hailed monsters and dined with ghosts."

She smiled at me, revealing a gap between her two front teeth. She turned around and grinned broadly at the two women behind her who had yet to speak.

"Easiest thing to do," Margaret said, "would be to listen for the fetus. If the babe's far enough, we'll hear it, and ye'll be spared. If it's nae that far grown, then we'll have to remove it, and you'll be ta'en to the deadly nevergreen, 'm afraid."

My head whipped to Maura's direction to see her reaction, but she only sat there calmly with confident ease as Margaret crawled around

Maura on her knees to her stomach and placed her head on Maura's subtly protruding belly. I could not recall taking a breath during that minute she stayed in that position with her ear pressed against Maura's stomach.

Finally, she pulled away, saying, "yea, I hear a babe in there. I'd say yer about two-three months pregnant?"

Maura agreed with Margaret's claim.

"And, now onto the next lady—"

"She's not with Child."

Maura's sudden statement, though barely above a whisper, sliced through the air, drawing all eyes from me back to Maura.

"What d'ye mean?" Margaret asked.

"She's not pregnant," Maura reiterated. "But you are going to tell the court she is."

"Maura!" I yelled but she reached out to grab my hand, a silent gesture telling me to hush and trust her.

"You're not going against the court and their sentence," she explained quietly enough to not elicit a reaction from the disinterested guards. "You won't be sparing her, as you will neither spare me. You'll only be delaying the sentence until I give birth. Just say that she's not as far along with her child, that way we can say she lost it around the time I give birth, or at least until the moment I lose the babe as well . . . "

"Why?" Lady Sharp-Nose asked.

"Because," Maura looked at me, "I want

someone by my side."

The matrons stayed silent while shifting their feet nervously underneath them.

"Please. I'll be miserable if I wait all of these months alone," she paused before tagging along for good measure, "and as ladies yourselves, you know how hard it would be, especially for the babe..."

Margaret sighed and patted Maura's knee and stood up. She walked into a corner and the women followed suit. They huddled together in the corner and whispered among themselves.

* * *

"WHAT WAS YOUR MOTHER LIKE?" MAURA POSED this question over a lobster supper, a month since matrons had lied for us. After their secret whispering with a few sharp words exchanged for good measure, they came to a decision to help us. They left wordlessly in single-file, as the soles of their shoes patted against the smooth stone beneath them.

Margaret was the only one to say farewell. She smiled softly with her small mouth as her scarred cheeks curved like ruddy apples. I had a suspicion that she was the one who truly defended us.

("Are ye not a mother, Patience? Or ye, Prudence? Your little Mercy just bore a son last August. Would you wish this fate upon her? Upon him? Have some compassion, for Christ's sake.")

She may have been a God-fearing sort as a Scottish Presbyterian, but that still didn't stop her from loving the sinners and the saints by her own judgment. The Lord may have the first and final word, but she was the one who decided who was deserving of her time. She never mocked Maura nor me, refusing to call us anything other than 'Miss.' We had tried persuading her to drop the formalities, but she told us firmly how she reckoned that *nae'ne must've ever treated ye like a lady. Someone ought to.*

She was the only one we saw again who still regularly visited every few weeks, if only for an hour, as she was a midwife in Spanish-Town. She was a kindly sort with pale skin with thin blonde hair—not unlike how my own mother's hair had been—and beginning to bald in the back at her old age.

I finished chewing my piece before I tilted my head back, considering Maura's question.

"She was kind and loving. She wasn't a very good cook, but eating her pies is something that I dearly miss. She swaddled me in my blankets like a babe in every storm, even though she was afraid of the thunder more than me."

My smile dimmed as I thought of the whole memory of my mother. I never got to see my mum reach the early fifties that Margaret had entered. My mum was not of thirty-seven years when I last saw her, and yet she always seemed so, so much older. Her gray eyes grew duller and duller with every year.

"But she was quite scatter-brained, and I especially noticed it as I got older. She would talk to people sometimes when there was only herself in a room, but then the next day, she'd say nothing from sunrise to sunset and only watch me with wide, dry eyes. Then, one night, soldiers came into our house and arrested her for stealing from a . . . *gentleman client* of hers. And . . . I don't know what came of her after that."

"I'm sorry, Ann," Maura said to me, setting down her plate to sidle up next to me and put a hand on my shoulder.

"Maybe I'm not being fair to her. I loved her, and she loved me. She was just . . . messy, I suppose. We all are. Can't fault her for that. All I can do is love the little that remains of her, aye? That piece of her that lives on in my head."

Maura only hummed in agreement before returning her attention to her supper.

✳ ✳ ✳

"WOULD YOU SING FOR ME?" I PROMPTED MAURA who stood under the window, wrapping her hands underneath her already swelling belly. She was on the tips of her toes, peering through the bars at the palm tree tops that tickled the blue sky. She had spotted a nesting bird a few days ago.

I had stopped counting the hours, the days, the weeks as I had used to. It had made Maura nervous, not because it worried her, but because it made me fret. I tried my best to take every day as it came without dreadfully holding my breath.

Maura turned away from the sky and obliged me with a tune:

"The hours sad I left a maid
A lingering farewell taking
Whose sighs and tears my steps delayed.
I thought her heart was breaking,
In hurried words her name I blest
I breathed the vows that bind me;
And to my heart in anguish pressed
The girl I left behind me."

Maura had a silken smooth voice that ran through the ear like a river of honey. It wasn't angelic by any means; it was jagged yet soft like moss-covered stone, something imperfect but still sweet. Every word that fell from her singing lips was like a crystalized, glittering gem that grew unpolished from the earth. I never believed I deserved it, that I deserved her, but Maura tried every day to convince me that I did.

> *"Then to the east we bore away*
> *To win a name in story;*
> *And there where dawns the sun of day,*
> *There dawned our sun of glory*
> *The place in my sight.*
> *When in the host assigned me,*
> *I shared the glory of that fight,*
> *Sweet girl I left behind me."*

Our time at sea had felt so far away, felt so short. I still dreamt of it, and I dreamt even more of the crewmates that had passed on. Friends, they were fading in my mind. I couldn't remember the English twang of Handsome Dick's voice, whether Little Fen had a beard or not, what color John's eyes were, brown or blue, maybe even hazel. The details passed away before me, but I still clung tightly to the dreams I had of them, the sweet ones and the nightmares. I wanted to keep them alive for as long as I could, even if it was only in my mind.

> *"Though many a name our banner bore*
> *Of former deeds of daring;*
> *But they were of the day of yore*
> *In which we had no sharing;*
> *But now our laurels freshly won*
> *With the old one shall entwine me,*
> *Singing worthy of our size each son*
> *Sweet girl I left behind me."*

I couldn't always keep the darkness at bay. It would come to me, overtake me, and leave me silent and still on the cold floor. Some days I felt like I had gone mad, or like I had died already and was stuck in some Purgatory where I was trapped in stone for eternity. I tried to think of the life I still had, the laughter I had yet to share or the stories I had yet to tell Maura, but some days it wasn't enough. Some days I begged for death to come for me at last. But eventually, Maura would pull me out of the little hole I was hiding myself in and wrap her arms around me, and then I realized why I never wanted to let go.

> *"The hope of final victory,*
> *Within my bosom burning,*
> *Is mingling with sweet thoughts of thee*
> *And of my fond returning . . . "*

But I would have to let go. I would have to let her fall from my arms away into the inky abyss and dive into a pool of my own.

We were going to lose, we were *always* going to lose, and I worried that those few embraces wouldn't be enough to justify the loss, and that there was never laughter, never music nor song, never love nor light that lived after all, and there'd be nothing left to wake our deaths. And it all was meaningless.

> *"But should I ne'er return again,*
> *Still with thy love I'll bind me."*

But when Maura walked to me and kissed me on my cheek in the middle of her verse, it burned. That fire passed through my skin into my very soul where I knew the flames would rise and grow with every ember she breathed into me. That couldn't die, could it?

"Dishonor's breath shall never stain
The name I leave behind me."

* * *

"**D**O YOU THINK ANYONE WILL REMEMBER US when we die?" It was nightfall, but neither of us could sleep, so we just curled together in the chilling night-winds that come when winter turns to spring. Maura lay flat on her back in the stale hay as her arms snaked around her stretching belly.

"I'm not sure." Maura then paused before she turned to me in the dark; the tips of her long and outgrown ringlets that hung around her face glowed a pale blue in the moonlight. "Would you mourn me, Ann?"

"Every day," I answered without hesitation.

"Then I don't need anyone else to remember me. They can all forget me, for all I care, as long as I know I'll be mourned by you. That is better than a legacy."

❊ ❊ ❊

WHISKEY DRIPPED DOWN MAURA'S CHIN AS THE BOTTLE'S emptied contents mixed with the tears strewn on her cheeks. Her throat bobbed with the gulps of the liquor as her head was held up by Margaret's hand. Maura gave a yelp once the bottle was yanked away from her lips.

"Very good, Miss," Margaret said to her on her chipped wooden stool, tall enough to milk a cow, handing the bottle to her youngest daughter kneeling beside her. The elder daughter straightened the crude cotton cloth beneath Maura, as it was the best thing they could provide for Maura's lying-in.

Maura had drunk more than half of the bottle by now, and her eyes rolled around her skull as her head lolled to the side, but Margaret caught her by the nape and shook her slightly.

"Stay wit' us, girl!" she demanded. "We're doing all tha' we can. Arm yerself wit' patience and prayer."

Maura snapped awake, and she groaned as another burst of pain shot through her body, and she curled into her stomach, but Margaret used her free hand to push her onto her back.

"Keep her there, Miss Ann," Margaret told me. "Miss Ann!"

I was frozen beside Maura as I watched her writhe on the floor with labor pains. There was no apothecary to help (as men were forbidden by law to attend a childbirth, after all), no one but Margaret and her two modest daughters obeying her every movement. No other woman could be spared to help, no other friend was there alive to support.

This is how I watch her die, I thought. I had only watched one woman give birth at my mother's old brothel; the baby came out as still as a rock, and the woman died mid-wailing. They covered her pale body with the bloodied sheets of her bed, the only respect they could give her.

But what sheets would cover Maura's body? They didn't care. They'd probably be relieved if she died with the babe still in her. Save them from digging two graves.

Maura seemed out of her mind. It was as if she was possessed by some demon that wanted to crawl out of her mouth with legs like a spider. I could barely recognize her, even though I have been by her side for the past two days of this pain. God's punishment for Eve's sin, Margaret told me, as if that would serve as some comfort to me. No, I was certain God must have doubled the pain just for Maura, I could swear by it.

She was kept sedated by the whiskey, but

even that couldn't stop her from howling in pain. Margaret tried to shush her, telling her to restrain herself from those dreadful cries, but Maura screamed that she'd cry as *loud as she damn pleased.* That seemed to shut up Margaret. No one would hear her, no one could think less of her than they did already.

No one would cry for her if she died. Except for me. Even into death. Every day. That's what I promised.

Maura shrieked in agony and sat up, her eyes rolling back and her jaw stretching wide open to make a tunnel for the spiders in her stomach to crawl out of and eat all of us—

"Ann!" Margaret called me out of my thoughts. "Move yer bloody arse! Pin her down!"

I nodded out of my stupor and moved over to kneel behind Maura to grip her broad shoulders and pull her down to the ground, being as careful as I could. I laid her head down on my lap, and held her tightly, one hand on her shoulder and the other pushing away the baby hairs that stuck to the sweat on her forehead. Her eyes looked back at me from where she lay upside down, and that's when I found her once again beneath the pain and suffering. The moonlight from the lone window danced across her distant gaze, its pale blue rays darting in and out of her glassy eyes. One last tear spilled over and dripped down the side of her face and landed upon my thigh.

She gave into another convulsion as her

hips bucked forward beneath the blanket, and she grabbed my wrist and held my arm against her frail collarbone. I swore I could hear the muffled sounds of a baby's crying.

"The wee one's stuck," Margaret said to her elder daughter. "Prob'ly 'cause it's so early, poor thing. Hand me 'the secret,' Anna."

The elder daughter had a sack by her side, and from it, she produced a pair of long forceps. They resembled scissors with their handled hinges at the top, but their ends where blades would have been were made into flat loops that curved slightly like spoons to grab a ball the size of roughly two fists, the size of a baby's head.

Margaret then pushed Maura's legs back to make her bend at the knees. Then, taking the forceps, her hand disappeared beneath the propped blanket. Maura made a loud gasp.

"There's the head," Margaret said to her two daughters. "Get the water basin. Now, Miss Maura, m'dear, when I count to three, I need ye ta push as hard as ye can. Can ye do tha'? One . . . "

"Ann, take my hand," Maura muttered weakly into her chest.

"Two . . . "

"Take my feckin' hand, Ann!" Maura yelled with bloodshot eyes, her hand searching blindly for my hand on her shoulder. I grabbed it finally and entwined our fingers. I leaned forward, crowding her head with my body and vainly trying to bring her closer to me, like she was sure to slip through my fingers like golden ribbons of sand. I didn't want to let her go. Not yet.

"Three!"

Maura's groan came deep from her gut as she pushed with all of her might. When she deflated in my arms from exhaustion, she took shallow breaths when she lost her strength before Margaret started to count again. Maura pushed on command, and the spit from her hollering flew into my face in little flecks. I didn't look away from her once.

Around the seventh push or so, when the veins on Maura's temples seemed so full of blue blood as if they were to soon burst, a baby's bawl rang through the iron cell, playing under Maura's cries in a shrill harmony. Maura's eyes, clenched in concentration, shot open when she heard the new voice, and she tried to look past her propped legs to see her child.

"Settle down, Miss Maura, lie down," Margaret comforted Maura as she placed the forceps aside. "We just need one more push and that should do it." She placed both hands under the blanket and counted, "One, two, three!"

Maura used the last of her will to move the pressure through her body, and it came out through her mouth in a scream that made my heart rattle, teeth bared like fangs and dark brows furrowed; it was a face reserved for her most bloodiest of battles, and one I hadn't seen since we had been locked in there. Some part of me ran warm and soft at having been reunited with this part of her, this part that refused to die.

Maura collapsed in my arms the moment of her last effort, and we heard the baby cry once more. It was then followed by a moment of deafening silence when none of us dared to move. It seemed to last for eternity as we held our breaths in anticipation, waiting for the next move. Then, it was pierced by the babe wailing once more.

"There we go!" Margaret said at last as she brought a baby from under the blanket, wet and slick with blood and placenta, as it waved its chubby arms around. "It's a girl, Miss."

Maura, face somehow flushed and pale at the same time, looked away with glossy, dazed eyes and began to sob. The overwhelming exertion of the baby and her body spilled over with an emotional turmoil too great for her to bear anymore. Still, she found a way to smile through the tears, even giving a little chuckle that made my spine shiver with relief at the return of the Maura I fell in love with.

"Och, *fuck*," she whispered breathily, and laughed a little louder at her feat, grinning toothily at me. I smiled at her, too.

With a pair of scissors, Margaret snipped the umbilical cord and handed it over to the younger daughter with the basin. She dipped a thick cloth in the water and gently washed the babe with soft strokes. I carefully helped Maura sit up in the meantime, and I kept her upright by leaning her against my steady chest.

Margaret came around with the baby swaddled in a deep night-sky blue cloth and carefully deposited her into Maura's arms all the while saying, "She's healthy as far as me piss-poor eyes can tell."

An overwhelming tenderness flooded my heart as I looked over Maura's shoulder at the little one with her little arms tucked gently into the blanket. Maura cradled her carefully in her arms and pressed her close to her chest. I wondered if she could hear Maura's heart beat, and if it was as fast as my own. Maura was at loss of words, stumbling through her sobs and the smile that broke out on her face. She was as shy and incoherent as the baby herself, overcome with love and adoration. It was a side of her that she so rarely showed, even to me, and it made my insides melt into an indiscernible slop. I kissed Maura's temple, uncaring if Margaret and her daughters saw, for there was so much in front of me more important. Maura herself barely noticed. Her only response to my action was a widening of her smile. Caught in her own little world with her child, it landed upon me to make the introductions.

"Hullo, dove," I said to the little girl, and I delicately reached out a finger to her in greeting. The babe abandoned her crying for a moment to inspect my offer, staring blankly with round, beady brown eyes and an open toothless mouth. She responded in kind by tightly wrapping both stubby hands around my finger.

The tears began to trickle down my cheeks when I first heard her giggle.

* * *

"TELL ME OF THE GREEN FLASH, ANN," MAURA SAID TO ME in a hushed tone. She didn't want to wake the sleeping babe in her arms.

It had been about four days since she'd been born. Margaret had visited once a day to check on the baby and her mother, but she'd always kept her with Maura to nurse, as it would spell disaster to part the infant from her mother so early.

The birth had been reported to our keepers, and Maura was promised to be wed to the noose in two weeks' time, the next scheduled hanging. Margaret kept good on her secret and said that she would claim in a week that I had given birth to a stillborn so that Maura and I would be able to hang together. We were parting with this world, but we were leaving one new soul behind us.

I turned to Maura's gray, emaciated face beside me. She had taken a toll from the birth as she had already been unwell before, but now she was even weaker and frailer, breaking out in sweats and sudden cold aches. Margaret said this was awfully common, as the woman would become most vulnerable to the evil air after giving birth. There wasn't much to do except pray that it would pass.

But I couldn't help but be worried by the purple rings that circled her sunken eyes and the gaunt hollowness of her cheeks. The voice I had loved had lost that playful timber, choking into a dry rasp. The light in her I had worshipped before was growing dimmer and dimmer.

"Why would you want that?" I tucked a hair behind her ear, frizzy from the humidity trapped in the stone walls. It had grown down to her shoulders since our time in captivity. I didn't believe I would miss the short ringlets. "You've seen the real thing. What can I say to you that would be better?"

"Your wild imagination makes it better, Ann. You recite it like a great epic or a pain-staking sonnet to woo a lady."

"I do not."

"You do in my ears, at least. It's more personal because it's alive in your head, being played before you in a dream. It's your dream, it's all yours. And I want everything that's yours. So, tell me again."

Maura's cheeks tugged her thin skin into a small smile, and the embers of her special flame were still breathing behind her eyes, however smothered. I spoke without care to please her inquiry.

"Maura, have you ever stared at the sun too long?"

This was not what Maura anticipated, but it nevertheless made her chuckle dryly and carefully enough as to not break out into an awful cough.

"Och, Ann . . . maybe when I was a wee girl? But then I learned it was only too painful to figure out what the sun really looked like."

"Aye! When I was young, I too always stared too long at the sun. I was so drawn to it. You and I are the curious sorts it seems, Maura, even into destruction."

I ducked my head and smiled sadly. Maura couldn't see it.

"Yea, my eyes would burn, but I stared and stared at the sun until I could no longer, and then I'd blink the pain away. But, Maura, did you too see the green hue behind your eyelids?

"Aye, Ann."

"Oh, Maura, I live my life in metaphor, but there are no words that I could give to that color. Sometimes I don't even know if it exists. That maybe it's all in my mind. But . . . well, Maura, maybe that is what the green flash is like."

In gentle movements, I stood from where I sat next to Maura and her babe. A revelation was coming to me, and I was too stirred to sit still. Thus, I began to pace and speak whatever word entered my mouth.

"I've never seen the green flash and I never

will. And I've made peace with that. All I have *is* my imagination, Maura. It can be whatever I like it to be. I cannot picture what it actually is, but the green flash that exists in my mind is *mine alone.* Those fuckers out there can't take that away from me. And there, in my mind's eye, is everything ephemeral and fleeting from this world, and it all emerges behind the rays dispersing from the absent sun: there are the imperfect faces of our friends long gone, the curl of my mother's pale hair, the glimmer in your eyes, Maura, and all the things that will disappear in the time it takes to blink out the green. But I will know they were real. And just the sheer *possibility* that rests in my imagination, that *what-could-be,* oh, *Maura,* it has given me a hope hot enough to keep me alight all these months."

Every thought had been expelled from me, and there was nothing left hanging in the air between us beside my own heavy breaths. Grinning, I finally asked her:

"Tell me, does the imprint of its reality linger in your mind the way the fantasy does in mine?"

Maura stayed silent and averted my quizzical gaze. She grinned also, but in a way that suggested she was keeping herself from laughing.

Then, it dawned on me.

"Wait, have you been fooling me this entire time? Have you ever even seen it?"

Maura just shrugged, collarbones poking against her thin skin while she raised her heavy shoulders. Her grin was big enough to show her teeth.

"You bastard! Tell me!" I begged, easily kneeling before her and gripping her shoulder.

"I'll never tell," she promised, sealing it with a wink. "I'll keep you guessing long after my death. It's more fun that way with the mystery. Endless *possibility*, you say . . . "

My lips twitched as my smile wavered once I pondered her words. "After your death? What do you mean *after* your death?"

Maura stared at me, as still as a statue, and it was then I saw through the laughter and the smiles and I truly saw how tired she looked, how defeated. "I'm dying, Ann."

"We're both dying," I said dismissively, shying away from her uncomfortable gaze. "I thought we weren't going to talk about that."

"I can't ignore it anymore. This is . . . different. I'm dying *now*."

"No, Maura," I shook my head, "what are you talking about?"

"I'm not going to make it past this week, I don't think."

"No, you can't do this."

"Ann, don't be this way. I was going to die either way—"

"Do not tell me what not to feel!" I shouted in her face, my body shivering with anxiety and dread. The baby in her arms awoke and began to cry at the angry disturbance.

"All right, I see," Maura told me in between cooing and rocking the crying babe with one arm and placing the other hand on one of my clenched fists.

"You matter to me," I said to her, "*really* matter, Maura, I can't just . . . " I trailed off as I pulled away, tucking my arms around my middle to hide my hands.

"All right. But Ann, I might be dying, but you're not."

"What are you—"

"You're going to escape."

"What? What are you talking about? If I'm leaving, Maura, you're coming with me."

"I can barely move, Ann! Look at me!"

"I'll carry you if I have to—"

"You can't, Ann, and I'll die out there anyway —"

"Then I'll stay! We fought together, so we'll die together. That's what the plan was, right? Please, let me stay!"

"You can't, Ann." She brought a hand to my face and held my cheek, threading the tips of her fingers through the tangled hair above my ear. "You can't. I'm not going to let you pay for my death. I think at one point, I was selfish enough to have wanted you to stay trapped here with me. But it's different now. It's not just about us. You need to take the baby and run."

"The baby?"

"Yes, Margaret will help you, we discussed

—"

"No, Maura!" I grabbed her hand suddenly and pulled it to my chest, gripping it tightly with both hands as my tears dripped on Maura's blackened fingernails. "Don't make me do this. Don't make me live on knowing that I'm leaving you to die . . . "

"You have to. You have to do it for this wee one, Ann."

She looked down at the baby she was bouncing gently. Her eyes were squeezed shut as she screamed in confusion. I didn't want her to cry anymore. I wanted her only to be held tight and safe away from this life where she could live without knowing what it means to be alone and hurting.

"Don't let her be abandoned," Maura continued. "Let at least two lives be saved. Otherwise, yours, mine, and hers will all be lost. I'm sure of it. Give her a better life than we had, Ann. Make sure she is loved, loved in the way we never were. Please, I beg you . . . "

My heart had turned to stone and had sunk to the bottom of my being with the way Maura looked at me with such pleading desperation. Maura never begged for anything, to anyone. She was a proud sort, but she never let that get ahead of her common sense. She was just confident and so incredibly stubborn. She took life as it came to her and never looked back. She was quick with a plan and quicker with a quip, some scathing remark or light teasing that reminded me how laughter and smiling were just as important as the heartache and bloodshed. I admired her. I adored her. I loved her. I kissed her then, not knowing where to put all of my affections, so I settled for pouring them on her lips.

"I love you," I told her. I loved all of her, her entire being, the space filled on this Earth and never apologized for. I didn't know what I would do when that space would soon be vacated.

"I love you, too," Maura whispered back.

"So fucking much . . . "

"I know you do, Ann. I know. So, give all of that love to our child, please. And then give her mine, too."

We smiled at each other, like the world had disappeared and the sky spun around us, like we were twin stars shining alone in the darkness with a baby between. She had finally stopped crying.

The door rattled us out of our trance and Margaret was escorted into the room by the two guards. She had a burlap sack slung over one shoulder, and the small wooden stool carried under her left arm. She was a short woman but of a stocky build that only came from thick muscle built over years of hard labor.

Once the guards left her to do her *women's work*, she greeted the two of us with a cheery disposition:

"Good morrow, Miss Mary—*Maura*, and Miss Ann. How're we farin'?"

"It's happening today, Margaret."

"Oh. *Oh.* Yea, I see. All right." The moment her eyes widened with realization, she dug through her sack until she procured a small metal knife. "Yes, here we are. Have to use this times when the babe gets stuck to remove enough bone from that mother to fit the baby through, the poor dears. So, it be sturdy enough to do the trick . . . "

She brought the stool to the base of the singular window, our light during the past however-many months, all the while talking:

"Now, these bars have nae been replaced in decades, and the stuff that sticks 'em, the mortar, has been baking in the sun 'til it'll be nothing but a crumblin' dust. They've been bettin' on the height from the ground, the guards say. There's been talk among them of a new building yet ta come, but nae a'thing shall be done for another hundred years, I fare . . . "

She stepped aside and handed me the knife.

"Hop up on there, Miss Ann. I'm nae tall enough. Get the base like a chisel."

I stared dumbly at the offered instrument, like it was some key I had never thought I was worthy of. I blurted out:

"Why are you helping me?"

"We talked in the wee hours of the morn 'ere yesterday," Margaret gestured to Maura lying motionless on the ground as the babe blinked at her, "while ye slept. I was nae keen on it, ye bein' a felon an' all and lettin' ye go, but I don't really think yer evil."

"No," I blanched at her words, hanging my head low. "I'm fairly wicked, Margaret."

"Nay," Maura piped from the ground, quiet enough to ward off a cough. Her eyes were teary when they tore away from her child, but when she looked briefly up at me, she smiled without pain. "You're absolutely lovely."

She said it with such absolute conviction, like it was a fact as simple as the sun rising or setting, and it made me wonder for a moment if it was actually true.

"An' if I don't," Margaret continued, blind to the moment passing between the two of us. "The Lord only knows where that babe will end up. The orphanage is nae better than a prison. If she doesn't die here, she'll die there, ye ken. She's yer responsibility now, and I reckon that'll be good for ye. This is yer chance ta do some real good, Miss Ann. Dinnae squander it."

She placed the knife in my hand and ushered me to the stool. I stepped forward and began to scratch the mortar away. Some pieces broke away easily, others had to be chipped little by little. And when one was done, I wrapped my hands around it and pulled as hard as I could, nudging until it came away with my hand. I handed each iron bar to Margaret until I was at the last one, and Jamaica was laid out before me.

It had been so long since I had seen the world as it was meant to be seen. The grass, only a foot below the window of our underground cell, was green and healthy and swayed in the ocean breeze. Oh, and the breeze that had finally found my face! It was still a drafty, warm wind but the movement on my skin sent a chill throughout my body. And there was the tree, tall and gnarled that had most likely been planted there since the first colonists arrived, and in it was a nest of twigs and strips of palm leaves. And beyond was the grass and dirt and sand and trees, far from the scattered buildings—some being clean and cut with white stone with hints of gold and some being run-down shacks the rulers left abandoned for the poor—but in it I saw the future, and it was all beautiful. There was the expanse of freedom, clearer and crisper than any sparse sweet dream I could recall. And the limitless blue sky was stretched over my head. I felt almost dizzy looking at it, like I would fall into it.

The sight of the free world made me want to weep, but when I stepped down and saw Maura, fragile and limp on the ground, I realized that she would never be able to see the beauty of the world again, that she would be reduced to a skeleton lying on the prison floor.

But Maura didn't think of this like I did. She only smiled at sight of the illuminated cell and said, "now that those blasted bars are gone, the whole sun can fit through that hole!"

The sun was at an angle where it all fell upon Maura, cascading like a waterfall of light upon her brown skin, making it sparkle somehow. Her hair glowed in the rays, almost as if the curls in her hair perked up like freshly watered flowers reaching for the sky. She closed her eyes and basked in the light, leaning into it as it caught her and caressed her face. She beamed brighter than the sun itself, no matter how wide her thin lips could go. She looked as if she had never known suffering, like the only thing she knew how to do was to live.

I knew that whenever I would think of Maura, I would think of this moment when she outshone the sun.

Soon, the moment faded away, but I knew it would never be gone. It has burned into my brain where it will thrive in my memory, a golden treasure of my love. I knew even then that I would hoard it and visit it during the darkest of nights when the sun will no longer rise.

Maura withered back into her sickly self when I knelt close beside her, but she had enough strength to raise her child to her face. She rubbed her nose against the baby's, no bigger than a thumb. Maura giggled when the baby sneezed.

"Farewell, my little one. I wish you grand adventures with Ann. I know you'll be in good hands with her."

She reluctantly held out the baby to Margaret who patiently stood beside her, ready to bundle the baby in some other rags.

I beheld Maura one last time.

"Finally, you'll get some color on those

bones, aye?" She teased me while I kneeled before her.

"Oh, shut up," I tried to smirk, but it only came out soft and affectionate when I gently placed my hand on her cheek.

I leaned down, closed my eyes, and pressed our foreheads together. I wanted to remember this, simply being with Maura, and her being with me. It was the easiest thing to do, breathe her breaths and soak up her warmth. But the heat was cut through when a single chilled finger traced its way along my cheek, wiping away a hot tear. I opened my eyes at this movement, and said the last words I'd ever say to her:

"Goodbye, Maura."

"Goodbye, Ann. 'Til we meet again. Fret not."

I leaned over and pressed a chaste kiss to her grinning lips, light yet binding like a wax seal. I said nothing more when I pulled away.

I stood up and faced Margaret who stood with a puzzled look on her face, unsettled by our display, but she decided not to say anything and shut her gaping mouth. She nodded, holding the swaddled baby in her arms as I stepped towards the window. I stood on my toes and hoisted myself off the stool by the stony ledge of the window. My weak arms shook under my body's weight, but I managed to pull myself up to my stomach and crawled out of the hole, landing on the grass that I swore was softer than anything I had ever touched.

I turned to the hole once more where Margaret's red hands were lifting the babe to the window. As I carefully took the child in my arms, Margaret told me something about her faking a head injury to make it seem like I had knocked her out and escaped, but I didn't listen. I was tucking the blankets around the baby's face, making sure she was comfortable. Margaret gave me some words of encouragement or luck and I must have said something back. My mind was elsewhere.

As I began to turn and run away, a song trailed after my thudding feet that kicked up the dry dirt in brown puffs. It was a tune I knew well, but this time it echoed in the voice I loved:

"My Bonny lies over the ocean,
My Bonny lies over the sea . . . "

I ran away from that sirenic voice before the next words could lure me back to a rocky, crashing doom. I darted through the shadows, passing people until I reached the cobbled streets of Spanish-Town. When I had turned a hidden corner and paused to catch my breath, I looked down at the face of the babe I cradled in my arms. Her deep dark eyes glimmered in the sun as she took in her new surroundings, smiling at all the new things her life could now offer. I had seen that smile before, and I had loved those eyes.

That is when I realized what I was going to name you, dove. I was to call you Maura.

EPILOGUE

THIS IS THE END, DOVE. DEATH, MY OLD FRIEND, comes for me at last. He waits for me at the edge of my bed as I write this last farewell and beckons me with a skeletal finger. I have battled him many times before, but I am tired of the war. I have to surrender this time.

Now you know: of your mother, of me, and of yourself, my little Maura.

Your mother was a pirate, as fierce as she was beautiful, and she was the love of my life. She bore you on the gaol floor, and I stole you away as she lay dying. I named you after her, Maura. I wanted to look upon you, to call your name and call my love's in turn, as if I was calling her back from the dead whenever you came running into my arms. You are of her flesh and blood, and you kept my love alive. I thank you for that.

She was right. You are a blessing, a gift. And still, I consider you my daughter as much as you are hers.

I love you. So much. And so does she. Love can never die; it persists in the paper we write it in, even longer in the hearts we carve it into. Never, ever forget that.

But when this body dies, please, bury me with Maura in St. Catherine's Parish. We cannot be side by side, but our bones will be covered by the same earth, and I hope that it will somehow help our souls find each other.

There is fear in the unknown that stretches before us, but I have learned that there is also hope. Hope is what kept me alive then, and it is what will guide me into death now. It will hold my hand, and I will willingly let it walk me into the darkness. I fought for what I believed in this life, for my friends, for your mother, for you, and for myself. I have celebrated all I have done, and I have made peace with all that I couldn't. I am satisfied with that.

Let hope guide you now, and live beyond me, excited for what is to come despite the threat of pain. I regret the pain my passing my cause you, but never regret the joy we found in each other. I never did.

I visited your mother Maura's grave often at St. Catherine's, and I still never told you. I didn't know how to tell you any of this, and I confess, I was frightened to do so. I was worried I wouldn't do it justice, that I'd tell it all wrong, and it would be marred by my feelings. I now realize that the words I write can be just as important as the truth.

Sometimes I brought her flowers to rest against the stone as cold as her frigid fingertips had once been. Maura liked white lilies, she told me once long ago, with their dainty yet wide, pearly petals. Bring them to her every now and again, will you? Since I no longer can.

Don't bring me any flowers. They make me sneeze too much. But she will like them. Bring them for her.

You should be able to find her all right. The cemetery is in poor condition—not even nuns care much for convicts—but the name *Mary Read* is etched crudely on her gravestone. *Died the 28th of April, 1721. A Pirate.* That is all it says of her life. That is what they remember her as.

And they remember me as Anne Bonny. I couldn't care less.

When I die, bury me at St. Catherine's and mark me as Anne Bonny. I am sure someday, someone will find us, long since our bodies have rotted and our hearts have become the soil that feeds the scraggly weeds. They'll remember Anne Bonny when they see it on my grave, in the parish records, and I want them to remember the legend with that name, whatever it may be. Then, they will find Mary Read, *a pirate*. They will look upon us and despair.

They have a claim to our names, but that is not important. Names change with the wind; names belong to the namers, not the named. I no longer care for what I am named.

I only care for what I pass down to you, my dove. Your opinion is all that I need, and even though I lay dying, I know I will live again as who you'll remember me as; and there, in your mind's eye, Maura will live again too. And we will dance and sing and love each other in the green rays of the setting sun whenever you think of us again. And we will be happy. For it will be as what you dream it to be. For it will come from the tale I gave you.

That is our legend, in my eyes at least. It may not all be true, but it is real to me, and it will be real to you if you believe in it in some way. Cradle it in your hands, worship it, and love it like it were your babe, as it is now a legend birthed from your own mind.

Our legend lies with you, dove. Keep it safe.

AFTERWORD

This book originally began as a high school project. I have always loved historical fiction, and I wanted to write a novella to demonstrate the genre's power in adapting history, but it soon spiraled into something greater than I ever could have anticipated.

As a kid, I was obsessed with pirates. I was drawn to the fantastical elements: the adventure, the costumes, the swords, the magic. As I grew older, it became a steadier appreciation of the push and pull factors that lead to piracy in the first place. So, I thought it best to fall back onto my old obsession for this project, and my focus fell upon Anne Bonny and Mary Read. Their lives were so extravagant and outlandish, perfect for any novel, and I knew I would be able to adapt it easily since I knew the story of their lives well already.

Yet, the further I dug into their history, I soon realized that I never really knew them at all. No one did.

The 'Anne Bonny and Mary Read' legend as we know it today stemmed from a book colloquially called *A General History of the Pyrates*, written in 1724 by a suspicious and anonymous author under the pen name "Captain Charles Johnson." Beyond that, the earliest and *only* primary source on their lives came from *The Tryals of Captain John Rackam and other Pirates*, published in 1721, which never provided the intimate details that Johnson claimed to have been privy to.

Besides, Johnson's words seemed far too coincidental to brush off as being testified by unnamed *"living witnesses."* How could it be that they *both* were raised as boys, *both* went to sea over their love for a man, *both* birthed secret children they abandoned, *both* exposed their naked breasts to taunt their victims with their sex? They allegedly rebelled against the gender they were born into (safely justified by their forced upbringings, of course!), but they were constantly reminded of it and undermined by it in Johnson's narrative.

This only led me to one conclusion: Johnson made almost all of it up to shock and satiate his conservative, proprietous eighteenth-century audience.

More than that, this startling revelation became an obstacle: it also meant I had to scrap everything I knew and start this story from square one with *nothing.*

Yet, it was a blessing in its own way. It truly opened my eyes to thinking critically about *how* history was told and *who* told it with *what* motives in mind. History is always being rewritten and transformed into truth because it plays into an intended audience's preconceived notions of right and wrong, possible and impossible, who should win and who should lose.

In this Afterword, I cannot explain without a doubt the true history of Anne Bonny, Mary Read, and the rest of Rackam's crew. The dates, the charges, and the names mentioned in *The Tryals of John Rackam* seemed to be the most legitimate source of fact regarding their lives. Then again, even the truth of a court recording can be stretched in the name of propaganda. But, since that was the only source I could base anything off of, I tried to follow the events of that court trial as closely as I could.

There is no objective truth, only what we "know." You will have to determine for yourself what you believe. You can imagine a world where the events of this book happened as I wrote them, or you can research yourself and form your own conclusions. They may not be "true," but there will be "truth" *in* them. Your perspective shapes the world around you, and that means something. That means everything.

ACKNOWLEDGEMENTS

This book could not have happened without the access to important research, constant peer review, and the love of the wonderful people in my life. I will do my best to honor those whose work and support were absolutely invaluable to this story.

Thank you, first, to the National Library of Jamaica. This may be an odd start to the acknowledgements, but without the digital scanned copy of the original 1721 publication of *The Tryals of Captain John Rackam*, I would have never have been able to create a true (enough) basis of facts from Bonny and Read's trials or give life to the flat names of the people that made up their crew.

Thank you to Lee Bienkowski who, in 2000, compiled a list of eighteenth-century slang on the internet. It allowed me to immerse my readers by using words contemporary to the time period and now forgotten today. Plus, I find most of them are very funny.

Thank you to Sally O'Driscoll whose article *The Pirate's Breasts: Criminal Women and the Meanings of the Body* challenged me to critically analyze Bonny's and Read's distorted mythos through the lens of prejudice, inspiring many of the themes present in this book.

Thank you to Tyler Rodriguez who, in 2022, uncovered the burial records from St. Catherine's Parish of Mary Read, buried on April 28, 1721, as well as those of an 'Ann Bonny,' buried on December 29, 1733. While it cannot be proven to be the same pirate Anne Bonny, it allowed me to imagine a world where it was.

I would like to also thank my high school English teachers who helped me during the beginnings of this project to look at this story from different angles. You all believed that I had potential and challenged me to be more than what I thought I could be, and I will always be grateful for that.

Thank you to all my friends who read over the bare bones of this story. Your laughter and tears strengthened my resolve to share *Our Legend Lies With You* with the world.

Thank you to Sheena for accepting the daunting task of helping me edit this novel. Your influence has strengthened my work, and your talent will never not surprise me.

Thank you to my family: to my grandma, who read the roughest draft in one sitting; to my dad, who *will* finally be able to sit down and read the finished project; and to my mom, who was my biggest cheerleader as the (tied) No. 1 O.L.L.W.Y. Fan.

Thank you to Hayden, the other (tied) No. 1 O.L.L.W.Y. Fan. Our six-hour long phone call where you read my manuscript through sobs proved to me that I did what I set out to do. And thank you again for the fanart you drew of them; I'll have it up on my wall for as long as we are friends—which will be forever, or at least something very close to that.

And thank you to Anne Bonny and Mary Read, whoever you truly were. I hope there's a glimpse of truth about your lives within my novel. Or, at least, I hope you would have liked what I wrote about you.

www.ingramcontent.com/pod-product-compliance
Lightning Source LLC
Chambersburg PA
CBHW050837180626

46814CB00007B/2497